生活中、工作上，
用英文寫E-mail總讓你腦筋一片空白？

動動手指，只要短短幾秒，
就是一篇文情並茂的英文E-mail！

User's guide 使用說明

生活中看似簡單的一般交際，換成英文卻難上加難……

別猶豫了！在這個國際化的年代，英文E-mail就是走向世界的第一步！抄來抄去就抄這些！超貼心4大POINT，扭轉你的人生！

Contents 目錄

→ 貼心POINT 1

收錄77大真的用得到的 E-mail情境，生活&職場全都包！

想要申請學校？邀請人家來家裡開趴？恭喜其實沒那麼熟的朋友新婚？這些書中肯定會碰上的事情，這本書裡都有！

→ 貼心POINT 2

範例E-mail隨你抄，中文&英文齊對照！

不知道英文E-mail怎麼開頭收尾才得體，多希望有人幫你寫一篇供參考？沒問題！本書77大情境，每個都寫一篇E-mail給你看！並搭配中文翻譯，超級一目了然，甚至想要直接抄來用都可以！

懶人最愛超加分！

英打超慢的你、手指關節痛的你、純粹懶惰的你，就用這本書的貼心光碟！內含全書英文E-mail範文word檔，複製貼上就能使用，有沒有這麼簡單！

1-1 邀請參加聚會活動

From fiona@mail.com
To bob@mail.com
Subject Party Invitation

Dear Bob,

Tom and I have recently ¹ moved to Si and would like to invite all of our frie for a housewarming ² party.

Please join us at 16:00 p.m. on Sund 29ᵗʰ. Directions ³ are enclosed ⁴. If to come by train, please remember one train stops at our town each ho would have to check the schedule want to arrive on time.

We would be excited if you and you make it to our party.

Yours truly,
Fiona

文法重點解析

例句 1

at 16:00 p.m. on Sunday, June 29th

是說「幾點幾分」的時候，前面的介系詞通常是用at。例如我們會說at 3 o'clock（在三點）、at 6:30（在六點半）等。但在說日期、星期的時候，前面的介系詞則通常要用on，例如我們會說on Saturday（在星期六）、on June 29th（在6月29日）等。

解析單字 2

make it

make it 是個很常用的片語，在這封信中它的意思是「能夠（前來參加派對）」，這個片語含有的「能夠做到某事」、「達成某事」的意思，來看幾個例子：

► She can't make it to the meeting.
她沒辦法去開會。
► The hiker didn't make it to the top of the mountain.
那個登山者沒有辦法爬到山頂。
► I finally made it to the finish line.
我終於抵達終點線了。

以下還有一些「邀請參加聚會活動」常用的例句供您參考，也可以活用在你的英文e-mail中喔！別忘了，時間、人名等等的地方要換成符合自己狀況的單字或句子。

① I would like to invite you to our party.
我想邀請你來參加我們的派對。

② Could you join us this Friday night?
你這禮拜五晚上可以加入我們嗎？

③ Let me know if you can come.
請讓我知你你是否能來。

④ Information on transportation is enclosed.
交通資訊已經附上了。

⑤ Kindly respond on or before December 10th.
請於12月10日前回覆。

⑥ Please let us know whether you can come before next Sunday, March 17th.
下週日3月17日之前，請讓我們知道您是否能來。

⑦ Please inform us first if you would like to bring extra guests.
如果您要帶更多客人，請先通知我們。

017

貼心POINT 3

用字遣詞重點詳細解釋，文法&片語通通有！

人生如戰場，英文E-mail不但要能夠清楚表達意思，更重要的是要能巧妙誘導收信者往某個對己方有利的方向去想。因此，信中要用哪些文法句型、哪些片語，就變成攸關利益的重要選擇！你想要有心機地推卸責任，卻又不想被看出？你想要放低身段，卻不太懂得怎麼超級客氣地使用英文？就讓這些詳細的文法重點成為你的好幫手，讓你在信中注入各種小小的心機！

貼心POINT 4

各個情境適時補充，單字&好用句為你充電！

書中為77大情境各補充了相關的句子，較難的單字也列出整理，將這些相關的字句排列組合使用，想必就能寫出最為你量身打造的英文E-mail！

抄來抄去都抄這些！一邀請篇

最近剛剛到上海，想邀請所有的朋友們家參加喬遷派對。

時間是6月29號星期日下午4點，附上地圖，如果打算搭火車來，請記得我們離鎮很近，只有一班火車會停，所以如果您想要參加，要先確認一下時刻表。

與您的妻子能夠來參加派對，我們一心。

敬上

抄來抄去都抄這些！關鍵單字

① recently [ˈrisntlɪ] 副詞 最近
② housewarming [ˈhaʊs͵wɔrmɪŋ] 名詞 喬遷派對
③ directions [dəˈrɛkʃənz] 名詞 指示
④ enclosed [ɪnˈklozd] 形容詞 附上的

015

Preface 作者序

在這個網際網路當道的時代，滑手機已經不再是少數人的專利，無論是你8歲大的兒子還是你88歲的爺爺，都能夠輕鬆遨遊網路世界。自然地，過去需要靠著傳統信件聯絡的事項，現在也都能靠著電子郵件達成了。像是網路訂貨、寄送邀請、恭賀祝福這些生活常見的大小事，不再需要跑郵局、找郵筒，只要動動手指，就能夠輕鬆地把訊息送到遙遠的世界另一端。因此，懂得如何寫一封清楚的E-mail就是現代人不可或缺的技能了！

網際網路當道造成的另一個影響，就是全球各地的距離都彷彿縮短了。與世界各地的朋友聊天變得容易，跟世界各地的客戶做生意也不再像以前一樣費時費力。然而，畢竟並非全世界都會說我們的語言，因此，我們不但要懂得如何寫E-mail，更要懂如何用國際語言英文寫E-mail！

想到這點，你就開始頭痛了嗎？你並不寂寞，我有很多學生也是聽到英文E-mail就開

始擔心這擔心那，光是第一句該怎麼開頭就要苦思一天。曾有一次出過作業，要學生們寫一封英文E-mail給朋友，想不到同學們都紛紛埋怨：「E-mail好難，不知道怎麼寫才禮貌，論說文都比較簡單。」欸，同學們，和論說文比起來，明明是E-mail比較生活化啊！現在和親朋好友溝通都常常需要用到E-mail，而職場上更不用說，我可是有很多學生後來畢業進入職場後，都跑來和我訴苦，說工作上常會寫到英文E-mail，讓他們無所適從呢。

我身為大家的英文老師，同時也希望成為大家的人生導師，學生們就算畢業了還是我的學生，我怎麼忍心看他們被英文E-mail搞得慘兮兮呢？於是，這本可以「隨抄隨用」的書就誕生了。裡面列出了77種生活中、甚至職場上可以用到的英文E-mail範本，懶惰的人可以直接抄來用（甚至連打字都懶的話，也可以從隨書附贈的光碟中直接複製貼上使用），比較不懶惰的人則可以運用E-mail範本，搭配我在各個情境中列出的補充好用句以及相關單字，拼

湊出一份屬於自己的英文E-mail。省時省力，安心放心，英文E-mail不再會是你的惡夢了！

當然，E-mail是人與人之間的橋樑，而任何牽涉到「人」的東西，都不會完全地客觀，肯定會醞釀一點情緒在裡面。例如若你要寫道歉的E-mail，口氣肯定不會是理直氣壯的；若你想要催促別人快點繳交東西，自然就要將E-mail寫得一副火燒屁股的樣子，才能達到逼迫對方的效果。因此，這本書裡面若範例E-mail中運用了一些巧妙引導收信人配合的「小心機」，或一些能夠微妙地改變說話語氣的文法句型，我也會指出來和大家說明喔！這樣大家以後也能一邊寫E-mail一邊耍心機啦。

這本書送給我所有已經進入職場的學生們。一日為師，終身為父，即使大家已經在職場上叱吒風雲，還是我永遠的孩子，哈哈！希望這本書無論是在一般生活的人際交往上或是職場的聯絡上都能為你們帶來一點幫助。這是個重視溝通的年代，而擁有良好的英文E-mail撰寫能力，正

是與人順暢溝通非常大的一個助力。但願這本書的77個情境能夠讓大家熟悉英文E-mail的寫法，未來無論是遇到怎樣的狀況，都能夠清楚地透過英文E-mail表達自己的意思、情緒、態度，達到最有效的溝通。

說起來，寫這本書的過程中我開始萌生靈感，不但想要教大家寫英文E-mail，還想教大家在職場上怎麼靈活說英文、更想教大家怎麼在學校以外的地方使用一些學校不教的有趣英文會話。也許以後我會推出好幾集「一日為師，終身為父」系列的實用英語教學書喔，大家敬請期待吧！

Contents 目錄

抄來抄去都抄這些！

Unit 1 邀請篇

抄來抄去都抄這些！

Unit 2 申請篇

⊗ ▣ ⊖

抄來抄去都抄這些！
Unit **3 道謝與道歉篇**

⊗ ▣ ⊖

抄來抄去都抄這些！
Unit **4 通知篇**

⊗ ▢ ⊖

Unit 5 詢問篇

抄來抄去都抄這些！

Unit 6 抱怨篇
抄來抄去都抄這些！

Unit 7 恭賀與慰問篇
抄來抄去都抄這些！

⊗□⊖

抄來抄去都抄這些！

Unit **1** 邀請篇

1-1 邀請參加聚會活動

From fiona@mail.com
To bob@mail.com
Subject Party Invitation

Dear Bob,

Tom and I have recently [1] moved to Shanghai and would like to invite all of our friends over for a housewarming [2] party.

Please join us at 16:00 p.m. on Sunday, June 29th. Directions [3] are enclosed [4]. If you plan to come by train, please remember that only one train stops at our town each hour, so you would have to check the schedule first if you want to arrive on time.

We would be excited if you and your wife could make it to our party.

Yours truly,
Fiona

 打開光碟，複製貼上，
不用一分鐘，抄完一封信！

★套色的部分為關鍵單字，在右頁可以看到解釋喔！
★劃底線的部分都有相關的文法補充，請翻到下一頁就可以看到囉！

中文翻譯

鮑伯：

湯姆與我最近剛搬到上海，想邀請所有的朋友們來我們家參加喬遷派對。

派對時間是6月29號星期日下午4點。附上地圖。如果您打算搭火車來，請記得我們鎮每個小時只有一班火車會停，所以如果您想要準時到達，要先確認一下時刻表。

如果您與您的妻子能夠來參加派對，我們一定很開心。

費歐娜 敬上

Unit 1
Unit 2
Unit 3
Unit 4
Unit 5
Unit 6
Unit 7

抄來抄去都抄這些！關鍵單字　　⊗ ▢ ⊖

❶ recently [`risntlɪ] adv. 最近
❷ housewarming [`haʊsˌwɔrmɪŋ] n. 喬遷派對
❸ directions [də`rɛkʃənz] n. 指示
❹ enclosed [ɪn`klozd] adj. 附上的

文法重點解析

解析重點1

at 16:00 p.m. on Sunday, June 29th

在說「幾點幾分」的時候，前面的介系詞通常是用at。例如我們會說at 3 o'clock（在三點）、at 6:30（在六點半）等。但在說日期、星期的時候，前面的介系詞則通常用on，例如我們會說on Saturday（在星期六）、on June 29th（在6月29日）等。

解析重點2

make it

make it 是個很常用的片語，在這封信中它的意思是「能夠（前來參加派對）」。這個片語含有「能夠做到某事」、「達成某事」的意思，來看幾個例子：

▶ She can't make it to the meeting.
　她沒辦法去開會。

▶ The hiker didn't make it to the top of the mountain.
　那個登山者沒有辦法爬到山頂。

▶ I finally made it to the finish line.
　我終於抵達終點線了。

抄來抄去都抄這些！
補充例句

Unit
1

Unit
2

Unit
3

Unit
4

Unit
5

Unit
6

Unit
7

以下還有一些「邀請參加聚會活動」常用的例句供參考，也可以活用在你的英文e-mail中喔！別忘了，時間、人名等等的地方要換成符合自己狀況的單字或句子。

① I would like to invite you to our party.
我想邀請你來參加我們的派對。

② Could you join us this Friday night?
你這禮拜五晚上可以加入我們嗎？

③ Let me know if you can come.
請通知我你是否能來。

④ Information on transportation is enclosed.
交通資訊已經附上了。

⑤ Kindly respond on or before December 10th.
請於12月10日前回覆。

⑥ Please let us know whether you can come before next Sunday, March 17th.
下週日3月17日之前，請讓我們知道您是否能來。

⑦ Please inform us first if you would like to bring extra guests.
如果您想要帶更多客人，請先通知我們。

1-2 邀請擔任發言人

From nada@mail.com
To smith@mail.com
Subject Invitation to Serve as our Speaker

Dear Ms. Smith,

We are writing to ask if you would like to serve as speaker [1] on a media [2] panel [3] during the annual [4] conference [5] of the National Advertising [6] Directors [7] Association [8]. The media panel is scheduled to begin at 3 p.m. on Thursday, October 16, and end no later than 5 p.m. All of your expenses [9] will be covered by NADA.

We can think of no one more qualified to fill this role than you. We do hope it will be possible for you to undertake [10] this assignment [11]. Please let us know your answer as soon as you can.

Sincerely yours,

NADA Organizational [12] Team

打開光碟，複製貼上，
不用一分鐘，抄完一封信！

★套色的部分為關鍵單字，在右頁可以看到解釋喔！
★劃底線的部分都有相關的文法補充，請翻到下一頁就可以看到囉！

中文翻譯

親愛的史密斯小姐：

這封來信是想詢問您是否願意擔任此次全國廣告總監協會年度研討會其中一場媒體討論會的主講人。該媒體研討會將在10月16日（四）下午三點開始，下午五點前結束。您所有的費用都將由全國廣告總監協會支付。

我們認為您是擔此重任的最佳人選。真心希望您能接受這一邀請，並盡快告知我們您的答覆。

NADA主辦委員會 敬上

Unit 1
Unit 2
Unit 3
Unit 4
Unit 5
Unit 6
Unit 7

抄來抄去都抄這些！關鍵單字   ⊗ ☐ ⊖

❶ speaker [`spikɚ] n. 講者
❷ media [`midɪə] n. 媒體
❸ panel [`pænl] n. 專題討論小組
❹ annual [`ænjʊəl] adj. 年度的
❺ conference [`kɑnfərəns] n. 研討會
❻ advertising [`ædvɚ͵taɪzɪŋ] n. 廣告業
❼ director [də`rɛktɚ] n. 總監
❽ association [ə͵sosɪ`eʃən] n. 協會
❾ expense [ɪk`spɛns] n. 花費
❿ undertake [͵ʌndɚ`tek] v. 接受（任務）
⓫ assignment [ə`saɪnmənt] n. 作業；任務
⓬ organizational [͵ɔrgənaɪ`zeʃənəl] adj. 組織的

文法重點解析

解析重點 1

All of your expenses will be covered by...

cover是個很有意思的單字。一般而言它表示「覆蓋」的意思，例如用手把眼睛蓋住就是「cover sb.'s eyes」。在此處使用cover，表達所有費用都在該協會的「涵蓋範圍內」，一點不漏，讓對方感到安心，畢竟誰都不希望多花冤枉錢啊！

解析重點 2

We can think of no one more qualified to fill this role than you

句子的意思是「除了您之外，我想不出更適合擔此重任的人選」，也就是「We can't think of anyone more qualified to fill this role than you」，只是換句話說而已。這句不但巧妙地表達了「要是您不願意，我們會很傷腦筋，因為沒有更好的人選了」的意思，讓對方可能會因為心軟而更容易答應，同時也是拐個彎稱讚對方是這個領域的翹楚，讓對方感到開心而因此比較願意接受邀請。

抄來抄去都抄這些！
補充例句

Unit
1

Unit
2

Unit
3

Unit
4

Unit
5

Unit
6

Unit
7

以下還有一些「邀請擔任發言人」常用的例句供參考，也可以活用在你的英文e-mail中喔！別忘了，時間、人名等等的地方要換成符合自己狀況的單字或句子。

❶ Would you serve as our speaker?
您願意擔任主講人嗎？

❷ I would like to invite you as our speaker.
我想邀請您擔任主講人。

❸ We are prepared to pay all your expenses.
我們會支付您的全部開銷。

❹ We would be more than excited if you could undertake this job.
如果您能接下這份工作，我們會非常興奮的。

❺ We do hope that you could serve as our speaker.
我們很希望您能擔任主講人。

❻ We would be only too honored to have you as our speaker.
如果有您當我們的講者，我們將感到萬分光榮。

1-3 邀請參加研討會

From nssponsor@mail.com
To wang@mail.com
Subject Conference Invitation

Dear Professor Wang,

I am pleased to inform you that you are cordially [1] invited to participate [2] in the conference [3] on Southeast Asian Studies as our guest. Your round-trip plane ticket, accommodations [4] and meal expenses will be subsidized [5]. Should you be interested, please let us know at your earliest convenience [6].

I am looking forward to seeing you in this conference, and I am sure you will play an important role in the event. If your response [7] is consenting [8], I'll send the relevant [9] information to you.

Sincerely yours,
NS Sponsor

打開光碟，複製貼上，
不用一分鐘，抄完一封信！

★套色的部分為關鍵單字，在右頁可以看到解釋喔！
★劃底線的部分都有相關的文法補充，請翻到下一頁就可以看到囉！

抄來抄去都抄這些！英文E-mail生活必用──30秒抄完一封信！

中文翻譯

Unit
1

Unit
2

Unit
3

Unit
4

Unit
5

Unit
6

Unit
7

親愛的王教授：

很高興通知您，我們誠摯地邀請您作為貴賓，參加我們的東南亞研究研討會。我們會為您支付往返機票、食宿等費用。如果您感興趣，方便的話，請盡快與我們聯繫。

期待您能出席會議，並且相信您會在此次會議中扮演重要的角色。如果您同意，我會把相關資料寄給您。

NS主辦委員會 敬上

抄來抄去都抄這些！關鍵單字　　　　　　⊗□⊖

❶ cordially [`kɔrdʒəlɪ] **adv.** 誠摯地，友善地
❷ participate [pɑr`tɪsə͵pet] **v.** 參與
❸ conference [`kɑnfərəns] **n.** 研討會
❹ accommodation [ə͵kɑmə`deʃən] **n.** 住宿，容納
❺ subsidize [`sʌbsə͵daɪz] **v.** 津貼，補助，資助
❻ convenience [kən`vinjəns] **n.** 便利
❼ response [rɪ`spɑns] **n.** 答覆
❽ consenting [kən`sɛntɪŋ] **adj.** 同意的
❾ relevant [`rɛləvənt] **adj.** 相關的

文法重點解析

please let us know at your earliest convenience

這句的意思是「方便的話,請盡快通知我們」。
也可以用「please let us know as soon as possible」這個句型,表達「盡快通知我們」的意思,不過「please let us know at your earliest convenience」還是比較客氣些,因為一個是「方便的話盡快」,一個是「盡快」,前者似乎考慮到了對方是否有空,顯得比較貼心。

I am sure you will play an important role in the event

「play a role in...」是個常用的片語,表示「在……扮演一個角色」之意。可以真的用來描述在一場戲劇中扮演一個角色,也可以拿來當作譬喻用,表示某人在某個事件中「是個……的角色」。此處說相信對方在此活動中「將扮演舉足輕重的角色」,不但達到稱讚對方的效果,也能讓對方感覺到這場研討會中自己的存在似乎不可或缺,而興起答應的念頭。

抄來抄去都抄這些！
補充例句

Unit
1

Unit
2

Unit
3

Unit
4

Unit
5

Unit
6

Unit
7

以下還有一些「邀請參加研討會」常用的例句供參考，也可以活用在你的英文e-mail中喔！別忘了，時間、人名等等的地方要換成符合自己狀況的單字或句子。

1 I would like to invite you to participate in the conference.

我想邀請您參加此次研討會。

2 I look forward to seeing you in the conference.

我很期待在此研討會見到您。

3 I'm sure that the topics we cover at the conference will interest you.

相信此次研討會的討論主題肯定能引起您的興趣。

4 Your contribution to our conference topic will be very valuable.

您對此次研討會主題的貢獻將會非常有價值。

5 The conference topic is very much related to your current research interests.

研討會的主題與您的研究興趣非常相關。

6 We heard that you've done a lot of valuable research in this area.

我們聽說您在此領域做過很多相當有價值的研究。

1-4 邀請共進晚餐

From may@mail.com
To sarah@mail.com
Subject Dinner Invitation

Dear Sarah,

My husband and I are planning to hold a get-together dinner with some of our friends at 6:30 p.m. next Sunday, on the eleventh floor of the Emperor [1] Building. We will be very pleased if you and your daughter could join us!

While this is just an informal [2] event, the restaurant has a <u>dress code</u> and therefore you're advised to not arrive in casual [3] sportswear [4] or jeans. We hope to see you there! <u>I'm sure we would have a most wonderful evening together.</u>

Yours cordially,
May

打開光碟,複製貼上,
不用一分鐘,抄完一封信!

★套色的部分為關鍵單字,在右頁可以看到解釋喔!
★劃底線的部分都有相關的文法補充,請翻到下一頁就可以看到囉!

中文翻譯

Unit
1

Unit
2

Unit
3

Unit
4

Unit
5

Unit
6

Unit
7

親愛的莎拉：

我的丈夫與我將要在下星期日晚上六點半於帝王大廈十一樓與一些朋友們舉辦晚間聚餐。如果您與您女兒能夠參加，我們將會非常開心！

雖然這是非正式的活動，但餐廳有服裝規定，所以建議您不要穿休閒的運動裝或牛仔褲來。希望到時候能夠見到你們！相信我們一定會一起度過愉快的一晚。

誠摯地，
梅

抄來抄去都抄這些！關鍵單字　　　　⊗◻⊖

❶ emperor [`ɛmpərə] **n.** 帝王
❷ informal [ɪn`fɔrml] **adj.** 非正式的
❸ casual [`kæʒʊəl] **adj.** 輕鬆休閒的，一般的
❹ sportswear [`sports͵wɛr] **n.** 運動服裝

文法重點解析

解析重點 1

dress code

dress code指的是「服裝規定」，無論是職場或是餐廳、宴會場合等，都有可能會有dress code。舉例來說，smart casual、business casual、semi-formal等都是服裝規定的種類，而其中光是business casual又可以分好幾種，要是一一介紹可是說也說不完，建議可以上網搜尋「dress code list」，看看各種服裝規定的詳細說明。

解析重點 2

I'm sure we would have a most wonderful evening together

直翻意思就是「我很確定，我們會一起度過一個最愉快的夜晚」。但對方根本都還沒答應要來，怎麼就已經說「我很確定」了呢？原來這封E-mail善用了「I'm sure...」句型，表示寫信者已經擅自假設收信者「一定」會來，讓收信者覺得「哎呀，他都說『確定』我會去了，我怎麼好意思不去呢」而糊裡糊塗就答應邀請，是個增加說服力的小心機。

抄來抄去都抄這些！
補充例句

Unit
1

Unit
2

Unit
3

Unit
4

Unit
5

Unit
6

Unit
7

以下還有一些「邀請共進晚餐」常用的例句供參考，也可以活用在你的英文e-mail中喔！別忘了，時間、人名等等的地方要換成符合自己狀況的單字或句子。

❶ Would you like to come to our dinner party?

您願意來參加我們的晚宴嗎？

❷ I would like to invite you to dine with us.

我想邀請您與我們一起用餐。

❸ We do hope you and your husband could come.

我們誠心希望您與您的丈夫能夠前來。

❹ If you're up to it, we'll go karaoke-ing after dinner.

如果您想要，我們吃完晚餐可以去唱KTV。

❺ Please let us know in advance if there's anything you can't eat.

如果有什麼是你不能吃的，請提早通知我們。

❻ You are welcome to bring your family.

歡迎帶家人前來。

⊗ ▣ ⊖

From miller@mail.com
To customerlist@mail.com
Subject Invitation to our Anniversary Sale

Valued Customer,

We will be holding our 3ʳᵈ anniversary [1] sale next Monday till Saturday, from March 3ʳᵈ to March 8ᵗʰ. All items displayed [2] will be 20% off, and certain products will be buy-one-get-one-free. There will also be events such as lottery [3] draws for membership [4] holders and coupon [5] giveaways [6].

Please drop by the store and celebrate our anniversary with us! We will be only too excited to see you.

Yours cordially,
Miller Perfume Shop

打開光碟，複製貼上，
不用一分鐘，抄完一封信！

★套色的部分為關鍵單字，在右頁可以看到解釋喔！
★劃底線的部分都有相關的文法補充，請翻到下一頁就可以看到囉！

中文翻譯

Unit
1

Unit
2

Unit
3

Unit
4

Unit
5

Unit
6

Unit
7

尊貴的顧客，

我們下週一至週六（3月3日至8日）將要舉辦三週年慶特賣。所有展售的物品都打八折，而特定產品則是買一送一。還會有像是會員抽獎以及折價券贈送等的活動。

請到我們店裡來和我們一起歡慶吧！我們非常期待見到您。

誠摯地，
米樂香水店

抄來抄去都抄這些！關鍵單字　　　　　⊗◻️➖

❶ anniversary [ˌænəˈvɝsərɪ] **n.** 週年

❷ display [dɪˈsple] **v.** 展示

❸ lottery [ˈlɑtərɪ] **n.** 樂透、抽獎

❹ membership [ˈmɛmbəˌʃɪp] **n.** 會員資格

❺ coupon [ˈkupɑn] **n.** 折價券

❻ giveaway [ˈgɪvəˌwe] **n.** 贈送

文法重點解析

解析重點1

drop by

drop by這個片語表示的是「經過（某處）時，順便進去拜訪一下」的意思，並非「刻意去拜訪」。像是要去好朋友家玩時，因為感情夠好，不用拘謹地說visit（拜訪），而是可以用輕鬆愉快的drop by來表示。此處在E-mail中使用了drop by，也是想表達一種親切的態度，拉近與顧客之間的距離，要顧客不必刻意前來，只要經過店面時像回到自己家一樣進來逛逛就好。

解析重點2

We will be only too excited to see you

「too + 形容詞（或副詞）+ to + 原形動詞」這個句型的意思是「太……以至於不能……」，例如要說「我太矮，以至於騎不上腳踏車」，就可以說「I'm too short to get on the bike.」。然而有一種情形例外，就是前面加了only，並搭配「開心」一類的形容詞或副詞的時候，也就是這封E-mail裡用到的這種狀況！在這種狀況下，這個句型的意思不是「太……以至於不能……」，而是「非常……」，因此We will be only too excited to see you的意思就是「見到您我們會非常興奮」。

抄來抄去都抄這些！
補充例句

Unit
1

Unit
2

Unit
3

Unit
4

Unit
5

Unit
6

Unit
7

以下還有一些「邀請參加週年慶典」常用的例句供參考，也可以活用在你的英文e-mail中喔！別忘了，時間、人名等等的地方要換成符合自己狀況的單字或句子。

❶ As our valued customer, you will receive a discount on all products.
您身為我們尊貴的顧客，將會在購買所有商品的時候得到折扣。

❷ On our 3rd anniversary, we would like to thank you all for your unwavering support.
在我們的三週年慶，我們想感謝您一直以來的支持。

❸ All customers will receive a small gift.
所有來店顧客都將得到一份小禮。

❹ Please spread the word about our special sale to your family and friends!
請把我們大特賣的消息通報給親朋好友知道！

❺ If you have a membership card, you will get an extra discount.
如果您有會員卡，還能再打折。

❻ We would love it if you could stop by.
如果您能順道前來，我們將十分開心。

⊗ ▢ ⊖

From robin@mail.com
To cheng@mail.com
Subject **Proposing a Collaboration**

Dear Mr. Cheng,

I apologize [1] for sending you an e-mail <u>out of the blue</u>. I am writing <u>on behalf of</u> my company, Green Light Co. You may have heard of us— our commercials [2] appear regularly [3] on most major television channels [4] and radio stations. We specialize [5] in manufacturing [6] non-toxic [7] containers [8], and as we heard that your designing firm [9] provides [10] pattern [11] designs for all sorts of materials [12], we're proposing [13] a collaborative [14] project—we make the containers, and you give them a refreshing [15] new look.

If this idea sounds interesting to you, please let me know and I will gladly provide further details [16].

Yours cordially,
Robin Lin

打開光碟，複製貼上，
不用一分鐘，抄完一封信！

★套色的部分為關鍵單字，在右頁可以看到解釋喔！
★劃底線的部分都有相關的文法補充，請翻到下一頁就可以看到囉！

中文翻譯

親愛的鄭先生：

很抱歉這麼突然寄電子郵件給您。我僅代表我的公司綠光公司寫信給您。您可能聽過我們的事，我們的廣告固定出現在大部分主要的電視台以及廣播電台上。我們專精於製作環保且無毒的容器，而我們聽說您的設計公司能替各式各樣的材質設計花樣，因此想提出一個合作專案：我們負責製作容器，你們負責為它們設計全新的風貌。

如果您對這個點子有興趣，請通知我，我很樂意提供更多細節。

誠摯地，

林羅賓

Unit 1

Unit 2

Unit 3

Unit 4

Unit 5

Unit 6

Unit 7

抄來抄去都抄這些！關鍵單字　　　⊗◻⊖

1. **apologize** [ə`pɑləˌdʒaɪz] **v.** 道歉
2. **commercial** [kə`mɝʃəl] **n.** 廣告
3. **regularly** [`rɛgjələˌlɪ] **adv.** 固定地
4. **channel** [`tʃænl] **n.** 頻道
5. **specialize** [`spɛʃəlˌaɪz] **v.** 專精於
6. **manufacture** [ˌmænjə`fæktʃɚ] **v.** 製作
7. **toxic** [`tɑksɪk] **adj.** 有毒的
8. **container** [kən`tenɚ] **n.** 容器
9. **firm** [fɝm] **n.** 公司
10. **provide** [prə`vaɪd] **v.** 提供
11. **pattern** [`pætɚn] **n.** 花樣，花紋
12. **material** [mə`tɪrɪəl] **n.** 材質
13. **propose** [prə`poz] **v.** 提議
14. **collaborative** [kə`læbərətɪv] **adj.** 合作的
15. **refreshing** [rɪ`frɛʃɪŋ] **adj.** 令人神清氣爽的
16. **detail** [`ditel] **n.** 細節

文法重點解析

解析重點1

out of the blue

這個片語的意思是「非常突然、毫無預警的」，類似我們中文會說的「天外飛來一筆」。由於這封信的寫信人和收信人並不認識，之前也未曾聯絡過，突然來信就開門見山地說要合作可能略顯不夠客氣，因此才在信的開頭先為冒昧來信一事道歉。另外，由於雙方不認識，因此不在第一封信中就直接詳細列出所有合作的細節，而是於最後一段請對方有興趣的話就回信索取細節，也是表示客氣的作法，畢竟哪有人初次見面就強迫對方接受自己所有合作的條件呢？

解析重點2

on behalf of sb.

這個片語表示「代表（某人）」，例如說on behalf of my husband 就是「代表我老公……」的意思，而這封信中on behalf of my company就是「代表我的公司」的意思。由於寫信者和收信者並不認識，因此前面才需要介紹一下自己是「代表誰」寫信，並詳細介紹一下自己的公司是做什麼的。

抄來抄去都抄這些！
補充例句

Unit
1

Unit
2

Unit
3

Unit
4

Unit
5

Unit
6

Unit
7

以下還有一些「邀請進行合作」常用的例句供參考，也可以活用在你的英文e-mail中喔！別忘了，時間、人名等等的地方要換成符合自己狀況的單字或句子。

❶ I'm sure both sides will benefit from this collaboration.
相信雙方都會因這次合作獲益良多。

❷ It will be my pleasure to work with you.
我非常樂意和你一起工作。

❸ If you would like more information on our company, I'll be glad to provide you with some slides.
如果您想要更多關於我們公司的資訊，我很樂意提供您一些投影片。

❹ More information on our company can be found on our website.
想要更多我們公司的資訊，可以到我們的網站上看。

❺ If you're interested, we could arrange a date and location to meet and discuss further.
如果您有興趣，我們可以安排一個時間與地點會面，繼續討論。

❻ Please let me know if you have any questions regarding our company.
如果您對我們公司有任何問題，請讓我知道。

037

From linda@mail.com
To hester@mail.com
Subject Cancellation of Plans

Dear Hester,

I am very sorry to inform you that I have to cancel the dinner this weekend. I just heard that my grandfather is seriously [1] ill [2]. My husband and I will head off to see him at once, and will therefore have to move the dinner party to another week. Of course, you'll still be invited!

I apologize for the last-minute cancellation [3]. I promise that something like this will not happen again, and also want to thank you very much for your kind understanding [4].

Sincerely yours,
Linda

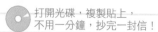
打開光碟，複製貼上，
不用一分鐘，抄完一封信！

★套色的部分為關鍵單字，在右頁可以看到解釋喔！
★劃底線的部分都有相關的文法補充，請翻到下一頁就可以看到囉！

中文翻譯

Unit
1

Unit
2

Unit
3

Unit
4

Unit
5

Unit
6

Unit
7

親愛的海斯特：

很抱歉必須通知妳，這週末的晚餐不得不取消了。我剛聽說我爺爺生了重病。我丈夫與我將立即出發去探訪他，所以必須將晚餐會改到另一個禮拜。當然，還是會邀請妳！

很抱歉最後關頭才取消邀請。我保證這樣的事不會再發生了，而且我也非常感謝您善意的理解。

誠摯地，
琳達

抄來抄去都抄這些！關鍵單字　　　　　×□─

❶ seriously [`sɪrɪəslɪ] **adv.** 嚴重地

❷ ill [ɪl] **adj.** 生病的

❸ cancellation [ˌkænsə`leʃən] **n.** 取消

❹ understanding [ˌʌndə`stændɪŋ] **n.** 理解

文法重點解析

at once

這個片語的意思是「立刻」。例如：
- ▶ You must leave the house at once. It's burning.
  你必須立刻離開這棟房子。火災了。
- ▶ The kids ran home at once when it started raining.
  一下起雨來，孩子們立刻就跑回家了。

房子火災、外面下雨都是很「急迫」的事情，迫使人必須立即做出反應，毫無拖延的空間。同樣地，這封E-mail中使用「at once」這個片語也是想表達一種「沒辦法拖延，我們必須『立刻』去看我爺爺（所以才不能如期舉辦晚會）」的無奈感，讓收信者更能理解其不得已之處。

解析重點2

last-minute

這個片語直翻是「最後一分鐘」，而它的意思其實就是指「事到臨頭了才⋯⋯」，此處就是表達「都已經到最後一刻了才改變計畫」的意思。收信者聽說計畫臨時改變，一定不怎麼開心，可能會想罵：「都已經最後一刻了，你才說要更改計畫！」於是寫信者乾脆使用「last-minute」一字自己替對方先說了，此舉反而會讓對方覺得「對嘛，你也知道自己那麼晚才講」，而心情平靜些。

抄來抄去都抄這些！
補充例句

Unit
1

Unit
2

Unit
3

Unit
4

Unit
5

Unit
6

Unit
7

以下還有一些「取消邀請」常用的例句供參考，也可以活用在你的英文e-mail中喔！別忘了，時間、人名等等的地方要換成符合自己狀況的單字或句子。

❶ I'm terribly sorry, but the party has been cancelled.

我很抱歉，但派對取消了。

❷ You are, however, cordially invited to our party next Saturday.

不過，我們還是誠摯邀請您參加我們下禮拜六的派對。

❸ I'm sorry about the sudden change.

對於此突如其來的改變，我很抱歉。

❹ We're sorry if this messes up any of your plans.

若打亂了您的計畫，我們非常抱歉。

❺ I'll let you know when the new date of the party has been decided.

決定了改期後的派對日期後，我會通知您。

❻ Please let us know if you'd still like to come.

請讓我們知道您是否還願意來。

1-8 更改
邀請內容

From amber@mail.com
To dan@mail.com
Subject Slight Schedule Change

Dear Dan,

I hope you haven't booked your train ticket for the party at the beach house yet, because we'll no longer be having the party there. According to the weather report, the seas will be pretty stormy [1] all of next week, so we're moving the party to somewhere safer, i.e. the Meridian Hotel (I'll send the directions [2] to you later; my phone is dying).

If you had booked your train ticket already, then too bad—however, we promise to make it up to you by treating [3] you to lots of your favorite wine. You're welcome to bring your own, of course.

Yours,
Amber

 打開光碟，複製貼上，
不用一分鐘，抄完一封信！

★套色的部分為關鍵單字，在右頁可以看到解釋喔！
★劃底線的部分都有相關的文法補充，請翻到下一頁就可以看到囉！

抄來抄去都抄這些！英文E-mail生活必用──30秒抄完一封信！

中文翻譯

Unit
1

Unit
2

Unit
3

Unit
4

Unit
5

Unit
6

Unit
7

親愛的丹尼：

希望你還沒有為了海灘小屋的派對訂火車票，因為我們不會在那邊辦派對了。根據天氣預報，下週整個禮拜海上都會狂風暴雨，所以我們將把派對改到一個更安全的地方，也就是美麗殿飯店（我待會再把交通方式傳給你，我的手機快沒電了）。

如果你已經訂火車票了，那就太慘了……不過，我們會請你喝很多你最愛的美酒來補償你。當然你自己帶酒來也很歡迎啦。

誠摯地，
安珀

抄來抄去都抄這些！關鍵單字

❶ stormy [`stɔrmɪ] **adj.** 暴風雨的
❷ direction [də`rɛkʃən] **n.** 指示
❸ treat [trit] **v.** 請客

文法重點解析

解析重點 1

my phone is dying

直翻就是「我手機要死啦！」，指的其實就是手機快沒電的意思。由這篇E-mail的口氣可以看出，寫信者跟收信者的關係不錯，應該是很熟的朋友，因此寫信者才會不避諱地指出自己正在用快沒電的手機發信給對方。這類的說法在一般朋友或比較輕鬆的工作場合都可以用，但若是重要公事上的E-mail，或是收信者正經又嚴肅，可就別邊寫信邊和對方聊自己的手機了！

解析重點 2

make it up to sb.

這個片語是「（做某事）補償（某人）」。雖然寫信者和收信者關係很好，但突然更改計畫，若沒做什麼事情來彌補，總是有點不太好意思。於是寫信者表示會請對方喝酒，雖然這或許並非什麼大不了的事，但利用「make it up to sb.」這個片語強調「補償」，對方的潛意識裡說不定不知不覺就會相信這真的是一種「補償」了喔！

抄來抄去都抄這些！
補充例句

Unit
1

Unit
2

Unit
3

Unit
4

Unit
5

Unit
6

Unit
7

以下還有一些「更改邀請內容」常用的例句供參考，也可以活用在你的英文e-mail中喔！別忘了，時間、人名等等的地方要換成符合自己狀況的單字或句子。

❶ I'm really sorry for the sudden schedule change.
突然改變計畫，我真的很抱歉。

❷ I hope that this doesn't cause you any inconvenience.
希望這沒有造成您任何不變。

❸ We will be moving the conference to a different location.
我們要把研討會改到別的地點。

❹ We're postponing the meeting to another time.
我們要將會議延期到別的時間。

❺ I'm letting you know in advance so that you can plan around the event.
我提早通知您，這樣您才能據此訂定時程表。

❻ I apologize for letting you know so late.
很抱歉這麼晚才跟你講。

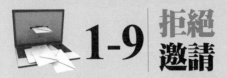

1-9 拒絕邀請

⊗ ⊡ ⊖

From rose@mail.com
To henry@mail.com
Subject About your Invitation

Dear Henry,

Thank you so much for inviting me to your family get-together next Saturday. I would love to go, but <u>unfortunately</u> I already have something else scheduled for that day: I'll be attending [1] the wedding of a college [2] friend as a bridesmaid [3]! Quite exciting, isn't it?

I hope your family doesn't mind me not turning up. Please let them know that I'll <u>definitely</u>[4] be there the next time they have a get-together[5].

Yours Faithfully,
Rose

打開光碟，複製貼上，
不用一分鐘，抄完一封信！

★套色的部分**為關鍵單字**，在右頁可以看到解釋喔！
★劃底線的部分**都有相關的文法補充**，請翻到下一頁就可以看到囉！

中文翻譯

親愛的亨利，

非常謝謝你邀請我參加你們家族下禮拜六的聚會。我是很想去，但不幸地我當天已經有別的事了：我要參加大學同學的婚禮，還是當伴娘喔！很令人興奮吧，對不對？

希望你家人不介意我沒出現，請告知他們下次聚會的時候我一定會參加。

誠摯地，
羅斯

抄來抄去都抄這些！關鍵單字　　✕ ⬜ ⚊

① attend [ə`tɛnd] **v.** 參加

② college [`kɑlɪdʒ] **n.** 大學，學院

③ bridesmaid [`braɪdz͵med] **n.** 伴娘

④ definitely [`dɛfənɪtlɪ] **adv.** 肯定地

⑤ get-together [`gɛt-tə`gɛðɚ] **n.** 聚會

文法重點解析

解析重點 1
unfortunately

字首「un-」的意思是「不、無、沒」，加在 fortunately（幸運地）前面，就是「不幸地」的意思了。不能參加對方的家族聚會，就算你自己覺得沒有很不幸，禮貌上還是要假裝很可惜的樣子，於是使用unfortunately這個字表達自己的遺憾。舉凡不幸的事都可以用這個字來描述。

例如：

▶ Unfortunately, the cake got stolen.
不幸地，蛋糕被偷走了。

▶ Unfortunately, John didn't pass the test.
不幸地，約翰考試沒考過。

解析重點 2
definitely

是「絕對地」的意思。既然這次「很遺憾」沒能參加聚會，下次就一定要到，於是使用「definitely」加強語氣。想要說「絕對……」加強語氣時都可以用這個字，例如：

▶ He's definitely not my brother.
這人絕對不是我哥哥。

▶ You'll definitely win the game.
你絕對會贏得比賽的。

抄來抄去都抄這些！
補充例句

Unit
1

Unit
2

Unit
3

Unit
4

Unit
5

Unit
6

Unit
7

以下還有一些「拒絕邀請」常用的例句供參考，也可以活用在你的英文e-mail中喔！別忘了，時間、人名等等的地方要換成符合自己狀況的單字或句子。

❶ I really wish I could go.
我真的很希望可以去。（但不能去）

❷ I already have a prior engagement.
我之前已經有安排了。

❸ Let's find another time to get together soon.
我們換個時間再聚聚吧。

❹ I already promised someone else to hang out that day.
我已經答應那天要跟別人一起過了。

❺ If you have time, perhaps we can get together sometime next week?
如果你有時間，也許我們下禮拜可以找時間聚一聚？

❻ Let me know earlier next time and I'll make sure to be there.
下次早點跟我講，我一定到。

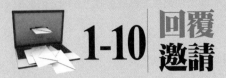

⊗◻⊖

From hu@mail.com
To li@mail.com
Subject **Accepting your Invitation**

Dear Mr. Li,

Thank you so much for inviting me to give a speech at the Chamber [1] of Commerce [2] monthly luncheon [3] at 11:30 a.m., September 21st, at the Mayor's Building. I am <u>more than happy</u> to <u>accept</u> your invitation.

I look forward to this opportunity [4] to further discuss with you and the members of the Chamber of Commerce on the subject of business in the next decade [5]. Thank you again for giving me the opportunity to share my ideas with you all.

Sincerely Yours,
Kate Hu

打開光碟，複製貼上，
不用一分鐘，抄完一封信！

★套色的部分是關鍵單字，在右頁可以看到解釋喔！
★劃底線的部分都有相關的文法補充，請翻到下一頁就可以看到囉！

中文翻譯

親愛的李先生：

非常感謝您邀請我於9月21日上午11:30在市長大樓商會的月度午宴上進行演講。我非常樂意接受您的邀請。

我很期待能有這個機會與您及商會的成員們進一步討論今後十年的商業事務。再次謝謝您給我這個機會，讓我能夠與你們大家分享我的各種想法。

誠摯地，
胡凱特

Unit 1
Unit 2
Unit 3
Unit 4
Unit 5
Unit 6
Unit 7

抄來抄去都抄這些！關鍵單字   ⊗ ▢ ⚊

❶ chamber [`tʃembɚ] n. 貿易團體
❷ commerce [`kamɝs] n. 商業；貿易
❸ luncheon [`lʌntʃən] n. 午宴；正式的午餐
❹ opportunity [ˌapɚ`tjunətɪ] n. 機會
❺ decade [`dɛked] n. 十年

文法重點解析

解析重點**1**
more than happy

在形容詞前面加上「more than...」，表示
「比⋯⋯更⋯⋯」的意思，例如more than happy
的意思就是「比開心還要更開心」。在此處使
用這個句型，就是讓收信人知道自己收到這個
邀請「超高興的」、「非常樂意接受邀請」。
類似的說法還有more than pleased、more than
excited、more than glad等等，都可以用在信中
表達收到邀請有多高興。

解析重點**2**
accept

表達「接受」邀請可以用accept這個字。和accept
很容易搞混的一個字是receive，它的意思是「收
到」，乍看之下兩者講的事情好像很類似，但也
有一些相異。accept指的是「心態上」已經主觀
地接受某物，而receive則純粹指「收到」某個東
西，但不代表心裡就已經接受了這個東西。

舉例來說，如果你收到了一顆炸彈，那麼就可以說
你「receive」了一顆炸彈，但不能說「accept」
了一顆炸彈，因為想當然你心裡是不可能「接納」
這顆炸彈的。而若要像這封E-mail中一樣表達接
受對方的邀請，則要使用「accept」，因為若說
「receive」，那只表示「收到了」邀請，不代表
就「接受」邀請。

抄來抄去都抄這些！
補充例句

Unit
1

Unit
2

Unit
3

Unit
4

Unit
5

Unit
6

Unit
7

以下還有一些「回覆邀請」常用的例句供參考，也可以活用在你的英文e-mail中喔！別忘了，時間、人名等等的地方要換成符合自己狀況的單字或句子。

❶ I would be delighted to accept your invitation.

我很樂意接受邀請。

❷ I was overjoyed when I got your invitation.

收到您的邀請時，我非常開心。

❸ Of course I'd be willing to go to the get-together!

我當然很樂意去參加聚會！

❹ Thank you so much for thinking of inviting me.

非常謝謝你想到要邀請我。

❺ I'm honored to have been invited.

能受邀，我真是太光榮了。

❻ I feel very flattered to have been invited.

能被邀請，我真是受寵若驚。

⊗▣⊜

From green@mail.com
To white@mail.com
Subject Thanks for your Invitation

Dear Mr. White,

I'm writing to thank you for inviting me to your dinner party last weekend. As you already know, I'm still new <u>in these parts</u> and am grateful ¹ for every opportunity ² to get to make new friends. <u>If not for</u> your kind invitation, I would probably have spent last Saturday night lamenting ³ my own loneliness ⁴ at home!

I'll be sure to invite you and Mrs. White over to my place someday for dinner, though I'll need to polish ⁵ up my cooking skills first!

Cordially Yours,
Jane Green

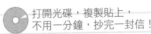

打開光碟，複製貼上，
不用一分鐘，抄完一封信！

★套色的部分為關鍵單字，在右頁可以看到解釋喔！
★劃底線的部分都有相關的文法補充，請翻到下一頁就可以看到囉！

中文翻譯

Unit 1

Unit 2

Unit 3

Unit 4

Unit 5

Unit 6

Unit 7

親愛的懷特先生：

我寫信來是要感謝您上週末邀請我參加您的晚餐派對。如您所知，我和這一帶還不熟悉，所以非常感激所有能夠交新朋友的機會。若沒有您善意的邀請，我上禮拜六晚上大概會在家裡哀嘆自己有多寂寞呢。

我將來某天一定也會邀請您與您的太太一起來我家吃晚餐，不過我得先練一下烹飪技術才行！

誠摯地，

珍‧格林

抄來抄去都抄這些！關鍵單字　　　　　　　×□−

❶ grateful [`gretfəl] **adj.** 感激的

❷ opportunity [ˌɑpə`tjunətɪ] **n.** 機會

❸ lament [lə`mɛnt] **v.** 惋嘆

❹ loneliness [`lonlɪnɪs] **n.** 寂寞

❺ polish [`pɑlɪʃ] **v.** 擦亮、使精緻

文法重點解析

in these parts

part是「部分」的意思，而片語「in these parts」說的卻不是「在這些部分」，而是「在這一帶」的意思。例如：

▶ There aren't many good restaurants in these parts.

這一帶好吃的餐廳不多。

▶ People don't carry umbrellas in these parts.

在這一帶，居民不用雨傘。

If not for

「If not for...」句型表達的是「若沒有……就……」的意思，後面通常會接假設語氣的句子，畢竟光是If（如果）這個字，就內含了假設的味道。例如：

▶ If not for the traffic jam, we would be home already.

若沒有塞車，我們早就已經到家了。

▶ If not for the fire department, the house would have burned down.

若沒有消防隊，這房子就會燒掉了。

抄來抄去都抄這些！
補充例句

Unit
1

Unit
2

Unit
3

Unit
4

Unit
5

Unit
6

Unit
7

以下還有一些「答謝邀請」常用的例句供參考，也可以活用在你的英文e-mail中喔！別忘了，時間、人名等等的地方要換成符合自己狀況的單字或句子。

❶ I'm really flattered to have been invited.
能被邀請，我太受寵若驚了。

❷ Thank you so much for thinking of me.
非常謝謝您想到我。

❸ I really enjoyed myself at the party.
我在派對上玩得很開心。

❹ Thank you for giving me this chance to meet new friends.
謝謝您給我這個機會認識新朋友。

❺ I can't express my gratitude enough.
我怎麼感謝您都不夠。

❻ I would love to invite you over for dinner as well.
我也很想邀請您來我這吃晚餐呢。

抄來抄去都抄這些！

Unit **2** 申請篇

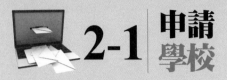

2-1 申請學校

❌ ⬜ ➖

From lin@mail.com
To brown@mail.com
Subject University Application

Dear Ms. Brown,

My name is Christine Lin and I'm very interested in applying [1] for your department's intensive [2] eight-week summer program. It fits my research [3] interests perfectly, as I have discovered through <u>E-mail exchanges [4]</u> with several of the professors in your department.

I have attached with this E-mail the required forms, my <u>Statement of Purpose</u>, and three recommendation [5] letters. Thanks for the help and please let me know if you have any further questions.

Best Regards,
Christine Lin

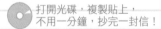 打開光碟，複製貼上，
不用一分鐘，抄完一封信！

★套色的部分**為關鍵單字**，在右頁可以看到解釋喔！
★劃底線的部分**都有相關的文法補充**，請翻到下一頁就可以看到囉！

中文翻譯

Unit
1

Unit
2

Unit
3

Unit
4

Unit
5

Unit
6

Unit
7

親愛的布朗小姐：

我叫克莉絲汀・林，我非常有興趣申請您系上的暑期八週密集課程。這個課程與我的研究興趣非常相符，這點我從與您系上許多教授以電子郵件聯絡討論後得到了確認。

我在這封信後附上了所需的表格、SOP、還有三封推薦信。謝謝您的幫忙，如果有什麼其他的問題，請通知我。

誠摯地，
克莉絲汀・林

抄來抄去都抄這些！關鍵單字   ⊗◻⊖

❶ apply [ə`plaɪ] **v.** 申請
❷ intensive [ɪn`tɛnsɪv] **adj.** 密集的
❸ research [rɪ`sɝtʃ] **n.** 研究
❹ exchange [ɪks`tʃendʒ] **n.** 交換
❺ recommendation [ˌrɛkəmɛn`deʃən] **n.** 推薦

文法重點解析

解析重點 1
E-mail exchanges

又可以說成「exchanges of E-mails」。指的是兩人（或以上）之間以電子郵件往返的過程，表示雙方（或多方）互相有通過信。申請學校時，一開始寄送申請電子郵件的對象很可能是系上一個專門負責處理學生事務的人，這個人不見得是學校的老師或教授，對系上到底在教什麼的細節也不見得瞭解，因此若已經和教授通過信討論過研究興趣，就可以若無其事地寫在E-mail中知會負責學生事務的人，這樣他對你可能會比較有印象。

解析重點 2
Statement of Purpose

簡稱「SOP」，不是工作流程的那個SOP喔！這個東西介於自傳與讀書計畫之間，不但要介紹自己，也要介紹自己未來的展望、為什麼選這所學校、進這個系想要幹嘛等等，旨在讓對方知道自己選這個校系是有目的的，而不是亂槍打鳥或因為聽長輩的話做出選擇（就算真的是長輩叫你選的，在SOP中千萬也別這麼誠實地說出來）。一般而言SOP不會寫得太長，要參照系上網頁的要求而定。

抄來抄去都抄這些！
補充例句

Unit 1
Unit 2
Unit 3
Unit 4
Unit 5
Unit 6
Unit 7

以下還有一些「申請學校」常用的例句供參考，也可以活用在你的英文e-mail中喔！別忘了，時間、人名等等的地方要換成符合自己狀況的單字或句子。

❶ I have heard a lot of good things about your department.
我聽說很多您系上的好事。

❷ The course list is a perfect fit for my interests.
課程表與我的興趣完全符合。

❸ I'm very interested in pursuing a career in this field.
我對從事此領域的工作非常有興趣。

❹ I have talked to some professors in your department.
我和您系上的一些教授談過了。

❺ Required test scores are expected to be sent to you in two weeks.
所需的考試成績預期兩週內就會寄送給您了。

❻ Enclosed are recommendation letters from my professors and employers.
附上的是我教授和雇主寫的推薦信。

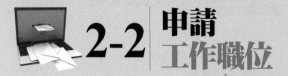

⊗ ▢ ⊖

From jackson@mail.com
To affleck@mail.com
Subject Applying for Administrative Assistant Position

Dear Mr. Affleck,

I saw your advertisement [1] on 114.com for an administrative [2] assistant [3].

I worked for a big multinational [4] company for one year as an administrative assistant and I believe that the experience has prepared me for the position you are looking for. I would be excited to be considered for this position.

Enclosed [5] is my resume. Thank you for your time.

Best Regards,
Jackson Lin

打開光碟，複製貼上，
不用一分鐘，抄完一封信！

★套色的部分為關鍵單字，在右頁可以看到解釋喔！
★劃底線的部分都有相關的文法補充，請翻到下一頁就可以看到囉！

中文翻譯

Unit
1

Unit
2

Unit
3

Unit
4

Unit
5

Unit
6

Unit
7

親愛的艾佛列克先生：

我在114.com網站上看到您的廣告，說要徵一名行政助理。

我曾在一個大型跨國公司擔任過行政助理一年，我相信這個經驗讓我有足夠的準備，能夠勝任您要找的職位。若您願意考慮用我，我會非常興奮的。

附上我的履歷表。謝謝您寶貴的時間。

誠摯地，
傑克森・林

抄來抄去都抄這些！關鍵單字　　　　　　⊗◻⊖

❶ advertisement [ˌædvɚˋtaɪzmənt] n. 廣告
❷ administrative [ədˋmɪnəˌstretɪv] adj. 行政的
❸ assistant [əˋsɪstənt] n. 助理
❹ multinational [ˋmʌltɪˋnæʃən!] adj.
　跨國的，多個國家的
❺ enclose [ɪnˋkloz] v. 附上

文法重點解析

解析重點 1

I saw yor advertisement on 114.com

要說「在某某網站上」，就用on這個介系詞，後面接上該網站的名稱即可。例如若你想說「在某個新聞網站上」，就可以說「on a news website」；若想說「在某個歌手的官網上」，就可以說「on the singer's official website」。應徵工作的E-mail中可以寫出自己是在哪裡看到招聘的資訊，比較可以避免唐突，對方也可以藉此得知自己刊登的廣告是否有效，是個貼心的舉動。

解析重點 2

look for

片語look for的意思是「尋找」。和也表示「找」的find有什麼不同呢？原來使用find時，一般而言是表示「找到」的意思，而look for純粹是「找」，不見得有找到。比較以下兩句看看：

▶ I found my glasses on the floor.
　我在地上找到了眼鏡。

▶ I looked for my glasses on the floor.
　我在地上找眼鏡。（不見得有找到）

抄來抄去都抄這些！
補充例句

Unit 1

Unit 2

Unit 3

Unit 4

Unit 5

Unit 6

Unit 7

以下還有一些「申請工作職位」常用的例句供參考，也可以活用在你的英文e-mail中喔！別忘了，時間、人名等等的地方要換成符合自己狀況的單字或句子。

❶ I have attached my CV.
我的CV已經附上了。

❷ I believe that I'm qualified for this job.
我相信我有資格勝任這個工作。

❸ Though I may not be very experienced, I learn very fast.
雖然我的經驗可能不算豐富，但我學得很快。

❹ If you would like to talk to my previous employers, I could provide you some contact information.
如果您想和我以前的雇主談談，我可以提供您一些聯絡資訊。

❺ I have always wanted to work in a company like yours.
我一直都想在您這樣的公司裡工作。

❻ I would be grateful if given an opportunity to have an interview with you.
若有機會能被您面試，我將感激不盡。

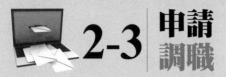

⊗◻⊖

From snow@mail.com
To chen@mail.com
Subject **Application to Transfer**

Dear Mrs. Chen,
This is Chrissie Snow from the Administrative [1] Department. I have been working here for 6 years. However, I regret to say that I'll have to move away in 3 months because of family reasons and therefore will no longer be able to work at this particular [2] branch.

As I love the company and hope to continue working with you all, I am requesting [3] to be transferred [4] to the Brighton branch, which will be quite close to where I'm moving to. I have talked to the managers [5] over there and they believe that such an arrangement [6] is possible.

Please let me know if there are any forms I need to fill out for this.

Sincerely Yours,
Chrissie Snow

 打開光碟，複製貼上，
不用一分鐘，抄完一封信！

★套色的部分為關鍵單字，在右頁可以看到解釋喔！
★劃底線的部分都有相關的文法補充，請翻到下一頁就可以看到囉！

中文翻譯

Unit
1

Unit
2

Unit
3

Unit
4

Unit
5

Unit
6

Unit
7

親愛的陳女士：

我是行政部門的克利希・史諾。我已經在這邊工作六年了。然而，不幸的是，我在三個月內因家庭因素將要搬家，不再能夠在這個分部工作。

因為我熱愛公司，希望能繼續與大家一起工作，我請求調職到布萊頓分部去，這樣離我的新家會很近。我已經和那邊的主管談過了，他們相信這樣的安排是可行的。

請讓我知道想調職是否需要填什麼表格。

誠摯地，
克利希・史諾

抄來抄去都抄這些！關鍵單字　　　✕ ▢ ⊖

❶ administrative [əd`mɪnə͵stretɪv] adj. 行政的
❷ particular [pə`tɪkjələ] adj. 特定的
❸ request [rɪ`kwɛst] v. 要求，請求
❹ transfer [træns`fɚ] v. 轉移，調換
❺ manager [`mænɪdʒə] n. 主管
❻ arrangement [ə`rendʒmənt] n. 安排

文法重點解析

解析重點1

I regret to say

「I regret to say...」這個句型直翻就是「我很懊悔地必須說……」，通常用於通知別人壞消息時。寫信者只是想調職，並不是什麼壞消息，但她使用這個句型，令對方覺得寫信者認為「因為搬家必須離開這家公司」是很令人難過的事情，藉此顯示自己對公司的忠誠與喜愛，是個帶點小心機的作法。再看看幾個例句：

▶ I regret to say that I don't remember what happened at all.

不幸的是，我根本不記得發生什麼事了。

▶ I regret to say that it's not possible.

不好意思，那是不可能的。

解析重點2

fill out

fill out這個片語用於表示「填表格、填表單」的意思，此外fill in也可以當作同樣的意思。不過，兩者相比起來fill in的用法比較廣泛，可以使用在表單以外的其他地方，例如若你錯過了某件有趣的事，但你真的很想知道到底發生什麼事，就可以找當時在場的人，跟他說：「Fill me in.」（把最新發展通通告訴我吧。）

抄來抄去都抄這些！
補充例句

Unit
1

Unit
2

Unit
3

Unit
4

Unit
5

Unit
6

Unit
7

以下還有一些「申請調職」常用的例句供參考，也可以活用在你的英文e-mail中喔！別忘了，時間、人名等等的地方要換成符合自己狀況的單字或句子。

❶ I would like to transfer to another department.
　我想要調到別的部門。

❷ I feel like my strengths and skills are more suited for the Sales Department.
　我覺得我的長處和能力比較適合業務部。

❸ I will continue to work hard and strive for perfection there.
　我到了那邊一定會持續努力工作、追求完美。

❹ Though I will be moving away, I still wish to continue contributing to this company.
　雖然我要搬家了，我還是希望能夠持續對這家公司做出貢獻。

❺ Transferring to the Shanghai Branch would save me a lot of commuting time.
　調到上海分部可以替我省下很多通勤的時間。

❻ Please let me know what arrangements need to be done.
　請告知我需要做哪些安排。

071

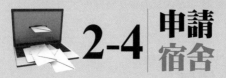

From alvin@mail.com
To wang@mail.com
Subject **Application for Dormitory**

Dear Mr. Wang,

My name is Alvin Lee, and I'm an incoming [1] student who will begin studying at FSU this September. As my hometown [2] is a ten-hour drive from the school, commuting [3] <u>is out of the question</u>, which is why I'm writing to request a dorm [4] room.

If possible, I would like to <u>room with</u> someone who's quiet and doesn't smoke. I would also like to have a room with simple cooking facilities [5]. Please let me know if any of these are still available [6].

Sincerely Yours,
Alvin Lee

打開光碟，複製貼上，
不用一分鐘，抄完一封信！

★套色的部分**為關鍵單字**，在右頁可以看到解釋喔！
★劃底線的部分都有相關的文法補充，請翻到下一頁就可以看到囉！

中文翻譯

親愛的王先生：
我叫李艾文，我是個將要自九月起在FSU大學唸書的學生。因為我的家鄉離學校要開車十個小時，通勤是不可能的，所以我寫信來申請宿舍房間。

如果可以，我希望能和安靜、不吸菸的室友同住，我也希望房間裡有簡單的開伙設施。請讓我知道是否還有這樣的房間可用。

誠摯地，
李艾文

Unit 1

Unit 2

Unit 3

Unit 4

Unit 5

Unit 6

Unit 7

抄來抄去都抄這些！關鍵單字 ⊗ □ ⊖

❶ incoming [`ɪn͵kʌmɪŋ] adj. 進來的

❷ hometown [`hom`taʊn] n. 家鄉

❸ commute [kə`mjut] v. 通勤

❹ dorm [dɔrm] n. 宿舍

❺ facility [fə`sɪlətɪ] n. 設施

❻ available [ə`veləbl] adj. 可用的

文法重點解析

解析重點 1

be out of the question

這個片語的意思是「不可能的」，在這封信中使用這個片語強調通勤「根本不可能」，因此「一定要有宿舍可住」。來看看幾個其他的例句：

▶ Walking all the way there is out of the question. It's too far.
一路走過去是不可能的。太遠了。

▶ You want me to lend you two million dollars? No way, that's out of the question.
你要我借你兩百萬？沒可能，我絕不會借的。

解析重點 2

room with sb.

大家常見的room是個名詞，但它其實也可以當作動詞使用喔！當作動詞時，可以是「提供住處」的意思，也可以像這封信一樣，當作「居住」的意思。room with sb. 這個片語的意思就是「與某人共住一個房間」，例如：I don't want to room with him.意思就是「我不想要跟他一起住一個房間」。在國內許多大學，有宿舍可住就已經謝天謝地了，不會特別想去指定其他事項，但在國外有很多學校宿舍都可以要求得非常細，因此你可以開條件，告訴對方你想要「room with」怎樣的人。

抄來抄去都抄這些！
補充例句

Unit
1

Unit
2

Unit
3

Unit
4

Unit
5

Unit
6

Unit
7

以下還有一些「申請宿舍」常用的例句供參考，也可以活用在你的英文e-mail中喔！別忘了，時間、人名等等的地方要換成符合自己狀況的單字或句子。

❶ Are there any dorm rooms left?
　還有剩宿舍房間嗎？

❷ Are the dorms co-ed?
　宿舍是男女共住嗎？

❸ I would like a room all to myself.
　我要一間自己一個人住的房間。

❹ Could we choose our own roommates?
　我們可以自己選室友嗎？

❺ I would like a suite with a kitchen and a bedroom.
　我想要一間廚房、一間臥室的套房。

❻ I would like to learn more about dorm facilities.
　我想進一步瞭解宿舍的設施。

⊗◻⊖

From yu@mail.com
To liu@mail.com
Subject Asking for Leave

Dear Mr. Liu,

I apologize for the sudden notice, but I'm sorry to inform [1] you that I won't be able to make it to work all the way through next month. I got into a car accident this morning, and broke both my legs. Thus [2], I have no choice but to ask for a month's leave.I promise to work extra hard after I get back to make up for the lost time, and am really sorry about all the inconvenience [3] that this may cause [4] you and the others.

Please see enclosed [5] a note from the doctor.

Sincerely Yours,
Nancy Yu

打開光碟，複製貼上，
不用一分鐘，抄完一封信！

★套色的部分為關鍵單字，在右頁可以看到解釋喔！
★劃底線的部分都有相關的文法補充，請翻到下一頁就可以看到囉！

中文翻譯

親愛的劉先生：

很抱歉突然通知您，但很遺憾地必須告知您，我下個月無法來上班了。我今天早上出了車禍，雙腿都斷了。因此，我別無選擇，只能請您准我一個月的假。我保證回來工作後一定加倍努力，以彌補沒能工作的時間。而且我也很抱歉為您與其他人造成困擾。

醫師的字條請見附件。

誠摯地，
南西·余

Unit 1
Unit 2
Unit 3
Unit 4
Unit 5
Unit 6
Unit 7

抄來抄去都抄這些！關鍵單字 ✕□—

❶ inform [ɪn`fɔrm] **v.** 告知，通知
❷ thus [ðʌs] **adv.** 因此，因而
❸ inconvenience [ˌɪnkən`vinjəns] **n.** 不便
❹ cause [kɔz] **v.** 造成
❺ enclose [ɪn`kloz] **v.** 附上

文法重點解析

解析重點 1

I'm sorry to inform you...

這個句型表達的是「很遺憾必須通知你……」的意思。雖然是不好意思的語氣，但使用了inform（通知）這個單字，可知寫信者是要「告知」對方自己要請假，而不是「請對方同意」自己請假。也就是說，無論對方同不同意，寫信者都還是執意要請假，只是知會對方一聲而已，這是個客氣但又堅定的說法。

解析重點 2

I have no choice but to...

這個句型的意思是「除了……之外，我別無選擇」。在這封信中使用這個句型，表達了寫信者無奈的心情，傳達出一種「我也是不得已的，我自己一點都不想請假」的語氣。看看這個句型其他的使用例子：

▶ I have no choice but to give him the money.
　除了給他錢之外，我別無選擇。

▶ I have no choice but to tell them the truth.
　除了告訴他們真相之外，我別無選擇。

抄來抄去都抄這些！
補充例句

Unit 1
Unit 2
Unit 3
Unit 4
Unit 5
Unit 6
Unit 7

以下還有一些「申請請假」常用的例句供參考，也可以活用在你的英文e-mail中喔！別忘了，時間、人名等等的地方要換成符合自己狀況的單字或句子。

① I would like to ask for a week-long leave.
我想要請一週的假。

② I won't be able to come to work tomorrow.
我明天沒有辦法來上班。

③ I'm sorry, but I'm too sick to come to work today.
很抱歉，我今天病得沒有辦法上班。

④ I'm asking for a leave in advance.
我要提前請假。

⑤ I apologize for the inconvenience my absence may cause.
我為請假可能造成的不便表示歉意。

⑥ I would have to take half a day off.
我得請半天假。

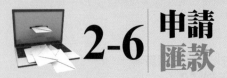

2-6 申請匯款

From ted@mail.com
To bank@mail.com
Subject Application for Remittance

Dear Huannan Bank, Dunhua Branch,

I hereby [1] **request** you to effect [2] the following remittances [3] subject to the conditions overleaf [4], which I have read and agreed to be bound by.

T/T   M/T   D/D

Date
Amount
Name of <u>Beneficiary</u>
Address of Beneficiary
Name of Remitter [5]
Address of Remitter
Remarks
Signature [6]

In payment of the above remittance, please debit [7] my account with you.

打開光碟,複製貼上,
不用一分鐘,抄完一封信!

★套色的部分為關鍵單字,在右頁可以看到解釋喔!
★劃底線的部分都有相關的文法補充,請翻到下一頁就可以看到囉!

中文翻譯

致華南銀行敦化分行：

本人已閱讀並同意遵守此頁背面所列條款，
茲委託貴行據此辦理下列匯款。

電匯 　　　　信匯 　　　　票匯

日期
金額
收款人姓名
收款人地址
匯款人姓名
匯款人地址
備註
簽名

上述匯款支付辦法，從本人在貴行開立的帳
戶中扣除。

抄來抄去都抄這些！關鍵單字　　　　　×□−

1. hereby [ˌhɪrˈbaɪ] adv. 以此方式，特此
2. effect [ɪˈfɛkt] v. 實現，使生效
3. remittance [rɪˈmɪtns] n. 匯款
4. overleaf [ˈovəˈlif] adv. 在背面，在次頁
5. remitter [rɪˈmɪtə] n. 匯款人
6. signature [ˈsɪgnətʃə] n. 簽名
7. debit [ˈdɛbɪt] v. 記入借方

Unit 1
Unit 2
Unit 3
Unit 4
Unit 5
Unit 6
Unit 7

文法重點解析

request

request的意思是「請求」、「要求」，和同樣有「要求」之意的ask很像。但不同的是，ask可以使用的情境比較廣泛，request則是在比較正式的狀況用。此處在跟銀行要求匯款，是比較正式的狀況，所以使用request。如果是日常生活中的小小要求，那用ask就夠了，例如：I asked my brother to take out the garbage.（我要求我弟把垃圾拿出去丟。）

beneficiary

beneficiary 有「受益者」、「受惠者」的意思，經貿術語中則是「受益人」、「收款人」的意思。除此之外，payee也有「收款人」的意思，例如：

▶ Is the beneficiary the same as the insured?
收益人和被保險人是同一個人嗎？

▶ Could you tell me how to spell the name of the payee?
可以跟我說一下收款人的名字怎麼拼嗎？

抄來抄去都抄這些！
補充例句

以下還有一些「申請匯款」常用的例句供參
考，也可以活用在你的英文e-mail中喔！別
忘了，時間、人名等等的地方要換成符合自
己狀況的單字或句子。

Unit
1

Unit
2

Unit
3

Unit
4

Unit
5

Unit
6

Unit
7

❶ I have read and will comply with all the
following terms.
我已閱讀並將遵守下列條款。

❷ I agree to be bound by all the regulations.
我同意遵守所有的規章。

❸ The transfer fee will be borne by the
remitter.
轉匯費由匯款人承擔。

❹ I confirm that I have read all the terms
and conditions.
我證實我已經閱讀了所有條款與規章。

❺ The account information is as follows.
帳號資訊如下所示。

❻ This is an application for remittance.
這封信是要申請匯款。

⊗▣⊝

From ben@mail.com
To commissioner@mail.com
Subject **Application for Trademark Registration**

Dear Commissioner[1] of Patents[2] and Trademarks[3],
(Corporate Name)
(State and Country of Corporation)
(Business Address)

The above identified applicant[4] has adopted and is using the trademark shown in the accompanying drawing for (common, usual or ordinary name of goods) and request that such mark be registered[5] in the United States Patent and Trademark Office on the Principal Register established by the Act of July 5, 1946. The trademark was first used on the goods on (Date); was first used in (Type of Commerce[6]) commerce on (Date); and is now in use in such commerce.

The mark is used by applying it to (manner of application, such as the goods or labels affixed[7] to the product). Five specimens showing the mark as actually used are presented herewith.

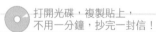

打開光碟，複製貼上，
不用一分鐘，抄完一封信！

★套色的部分為關鍵單字，在右頁可以看到解釋喔！
★劃底線的部分都有相關的文法補充，請翻到下一頁就可以看到囉！

中文翻譯

Unit
1

Unit
2

Unit
3

Unit
4

Unit
5

Unit
6

Unit
7

親愛的專利商標局局長：
（公司名稱）
（公司所在州或國家）
（公司地址）

上述申請人已經並正將附圖中展示的商標用於
（商品通用名稱），現請求美國專利商標局根據
1946年7月5日通過的法案而建立的商標目錄上註
冊該商標。

該商標於（日期）第一次用於該商品，於（日
期）第一次使用於（貿易類型），且現在仍在該
貿易中使用。

該商標採取（使用方式，例如在產品上附標籤）
用在商品上。現附上5份樣品，顯示商標的實際使
用情況。

抄來抄去都抄這些！關鍵單字　　⊗▢⊖

1 commissioner [kə`mɪʃənə] n. 長官，委員

2 patent [`pætnt] n. 專利，專利權

3 trademark [`tred͵mɑrk] n. 商標

4 applicant [`æpləkənt] n. 申請人

5 register [`rɛdʒɪstə] v. 註冊，掛號

6 commerce [`kɑmɝs] n. 商業，貿易

7 affix [`æfɪks] v. 使附於，署名，黏貼

文法重點解析

解析重點**1**
adopt

adopt有好幾種意思，包括「採納」、「收養」、「正式通過」、「接受」等，在此處意為「正式通過」的意思。通常通過法案、決議等可以使用adopt。請對照下列例句：

► After much deliberation, the manager decided to adopt her suggestion.
經理考慮再三之後，決定採納她的建議。

► He adopted the orphan as his son.
他將那名孤兒收養為自己的兒子。

► The agenda was adopted after some discussion.
經過討論，議事日程獲得通過。

解析重點**2**
herewith

herewith意思是「與此一道」、「同此」、「隨函」、「據此」等，一般並不常用，只會在一些非常正式的文書裡才會出現。請看例句：

► I send you herewith two copies of the contract.
我隨函附上合約書一式兩份。

抄來抄去都抄這些！
補充例句

Unit
1

Unit
2

Unit
3

Unit
4

Unit
5

Unit
6

Unit
7

以下還有一些「申請註冊商標」常用的例句供參考，也可以活用在你的英文e-mail中喔！別忘了，時間、人名等等的地方要換成符合自己狀況的單字或句子。

❶ The above identified applicant has adopted and is using the trademark shown in the accompanying drawing for alcoholic beverages.

上述申請人已經並正將附圖中展示的商標用於酒精性飲品。

❷ The trademark was first used on the product in October, 2007.

該商標於2007年10月首次用於該商品。

❸ The trademark was first used in textile goods on August, 2008.

該商標於2008年8月首次用於紡織品。

❹ The applicant requests that such mark be registered in the Trademark Office State Administration for Industry and Commerce.

申請人請求國家工商行政管理總局商標局註冊該商品。

❺ Please find attached examples of how this trademark is used.

關於此商標如何使用，請參見附件範例。

2-8 申請許可證

From li@mail.com
To ceca@mail.com
Subject Application for License

Dear President [1] of CECA,
I, Min Li, do hereby apply [2] for a license [3] to display [4] the trademark of CECA, "COOL" at my place of business located at 250 Felicity Street. This application is in accordance [5] with the regulations of the CECA.

I am cognizant [6] of the regulations [7] of CECA that govern the display of said trademark and the manner of conducting business, and I agree to abide [8] by such regulations at all times.

Sincerely Yours,
Min Li

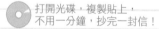
打開光碟，複製貼上，
不用一分鐘，抄完一封信！

★套色的部分為關鍵單字，在右頁可以看到解釋喔！
★劃底線的部分都有相關的文法補充，請翻到下一頁就可以看到囉！

中文翻譯

親愛的CECA協會會長：

本人，李敏，在此鄭重申請CECA商標使用
許可證，以便獲准在位於幸福街520號的公
司所在地展示「COOL」商標。本申請係依
據CECA條例提出。

本人清楚協會對上述商品展示和業務經營模
式的規範條例，並同意永久遵守這些條例。

誠摯地，
李敏

抄來抄去都抄這些！關鍵單字　　　　　　　 ☒ ☐ ⊖

1. president [`prɛzədənt] n. 總統，會長
2. apply [ə`plaɪ] v. 申請
3. license [`laɪsns] n. 許可證，證照
4. display [dɪ`sple] v./n. 陳列，展覽
5. accordance [ə`kɔrdəns] n. 一致，符合
6. cognizant [`kɑgnɪzənt] adj. 認知的
7. regulation [ˌrɛgjə`leʃən] n. 規則，規章
8. abide [ə`baɪd] v. 遵守，忍受

文法重點解析

解析重點 1

do

這一句其實說「I, Min Li, hereby apply...」就可以了，完全符合文法，這裡再多一個do的原因是什麼呢？句中不是已經有了一個一般動詞apply嗎？原來，在正式的信函中可以在一般動詞前面再補充一個do表達強調自己的意圖之意。此外，即使是在非正式的場合，如果想要強調「的確是」怎樣怎樣，也可以在原本的一般動詞前面加上do（或其變化型did、does）。例如：

▶ I do think he's gotten a bit thin.
我的確覺得他變得有點瘦了。

▶ She does look very angry.
她看起來的確很生氣。

解析重點 2

said

我們都知道，said是say的過去式，是個動詞。但在信中這個地方它卻當作形容詞來修飾「trademark」，這是怎麼回事呢？原來，said可以表達「之前說過的」的意思，因此如果你前面說過一個東西，後來又要再提到它，不想要再重新描述一遍，就可以用said來替代。例如：

▶ Jenny really loves her doll, even though said doll is old and dirty.
珍妮真的很喜歡她的洋娃娃，雖然那個洋娃娃已經又舊又髒了。

此句中的said就是用來指「珍妮很喜歡的那個洋娃娃」（而不是其他的洋娃娃）。

抄來抄去都抄這些！
補充例句

Unit
1

Unit
2

Unit
3

Unit
4

Unit
5

Unit
6

Unit
7

以下還有一些「申請許可證」常用的例句供
參考，也可以活用在你的英文e-mail中喔！
別忘了，時間、人名等等的地方要換成符合
自己狀況的單字或句子。

❶ I hereby apply for a food hygiene license.
本人在此申請食品衛生許可證。

❷ I am writing to apply for a parking permit.
我寫信來是要申請停車許可證。

❸ I was told that I couldn't take pictures
here without a permit.
有人告知我，我若沒有許可證，無法在此
拍照。

❹ I do hereby apply for a license to display
the trademark.
本人在此鄭重申請商標使用許可證。

❺ This application is in accordance with the
regulations of the CIMA.
本申請係依據CIMA協會條例提出。

❻ I saw on the website that I would need a
permit for this.
我在網站上看到需要許可證。

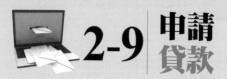

2-9 申請貸款

From green@mail.com
To bank@mail.com
Subject Application for a Loan

Dear Head of the Loan Section [1],

I am writing to apply for a 150,000-dollar loan from your bank to open a Japanese cuisine [2] restaurant.

The potential [3] Japanese food market is large in this area, and I believe that this investment [4] will prove to be profitable [5]. The money you loan us will be used on employment [6] of cooks and interior [7] decoration. My partner and I will provide real estate [8] that is worth 200,000 dollars as guarantee [9].

We await eagerly for your response!

Sincerely Yours,
Ted Green

打開光碟，複製貼上，
不用一分鐘，抄完一封信！

★套色的部分為關鍵單字，在右頁可以看到解釋喔！
★劃底線的部分都有相關的文法補充，請翻到下一頁就可以看到囉！

中文翻譯

親愛的貸款部門主管：
我寫這封信是為了向貴行申請十五萬美元的貸款來開設一家日本餐館。

這一帶潛在的日本餐飲市場非常大，我相信這個投資將會帶來不小的利益。貸款將會用於聘用廚師以及室內裝潢。我的合夥人與我將會提供價值二十萬美元的房產作為擔保。

我們非常期待您的答覆。

誠摯地，
泰德・格林

Unit 1
Unit 2
Unit 3
Unit 4
Unit 5
Unit 6
Unit 7

抄來抄去都抄這些！關鍵單字　　　　　　　⊗ ▢ ⊝

❶ section [`sɛkʃən] n. 區段，部門

❷ cuisine [kwɪ`zin] n. 料理

❸ potential [pə`tɛnʃəl] adj. 潛在的，可能的

❹ investment [ɪn`vɛstmənt] n. 投資

❺ profitable [`prɑfɪtəbl̩] adj. 有利益的

❻ employment [ɪm`plɔɪmənt] n. 雇用

❼ interior [ɪn`tɪrɪə] n. 內部，室內

❽ estate [ɪs`tet] n. 地產

❾ guarantee [ˌgærən`ti] n. 擔保

文法重點解析

解析重點1

prove to be

這個片語的意思是「證明是……」。通常會需要「證明」的事情，一開始一定會有人「懷疑」，不然就不需要證明了。因此，此處用這個片語，就是要表達：「雖然您可能懷疑貸款給我們是不是正確的選擇，但相信最後會『證明是』有利的」的意思，巧妙地藉由這個片語撫平對方的不安，並增加說服力。再看一個例句：

▶ The boy looked small and weak, but he proved to be very capable.

那個男孩看起來很弱小，但後來證明了他非常有能力。

解析重點2

We await eagerly for your response

eagerly是「非常期待、非常積極地」的意思。例如小朋友開禮物的時候期待的樣子、狗啃骨頭時興奮的樣子，就都可以用eagerly來形容。在這封信中最後用了這個方法收尾，就是想表達寫信者非常期待對方的回覆，期待得彷彿開禮物的小朋友、啃骨頭的狗。這是個能讓對方完全感受到寫信者期待心情的收尾方式。

抄來抄去都抄這些！
補充例句

Unit 1

Unit 2

Unit 3

Unit 4

Unit 5

Unit 6

Unit 7

以下還有一些「申請貸款」常用的例句供參考，也可以活用在你的英文e-mail中喔！別忘了，時間、人名等等的地方要換成符合自己狀況的單字或句子。

❶ I am writing to apply for a 100,000-dollar loan from your bank.
我寫這封信是為了向貴行申請十萬美元的貸款。

❷ I am applying for the loan to open a bookstore.
我要申請貸款開一家書局。

❸ It will be a great business opportunity.
這將是一個很大的商機。

❹ Please let me know how much is required as guarantee.
請告訴我擔保費用需要多少。

❺ I may have further questions on the details concerning interest rates.
關於利率的細節，我可能會有一些進一步的疑問。

❻ My business partner and I wish to apply for a loan.
我與我的合夥人希望能夠申請借款。

095

From abc@mail.com
To chen@mail.com
Subject Application for Opening an L/C

Dear Sirs,

Thank you for your letter on June 18th enclosed with details of your terms[1].

According to your request to open an irrevocable L/C, we have instructed[2] Mega International Commercial[3] Bank to open a credit[4] for US$ 50,000 in your favor, valid until Sep. 20. Please inform us by fax when the order has been executed[5].

Thank you for your cooperation.

Sincerely Yours,
ABC Co.

打開光碟，複製貼上，
不用一分鐘，抄完一封信！

★套色的部分為關鍵單字，在右頁可以看到解釋喔！
★劃底線的部分都有相關的文法補充，請翻到下一頁就可以看到囉！

中文翻譯

敬啟者：

非常感謝貴方6月18日有關條款詳細情況的來信。

根據你方要求開立不可撤銷信用狀，我方已經通知兆豐國際商業銀行開立金額為5萬美元的信用狀，有效期至9月20號。當你方執行訂單時，請傳真告知我方。

謝謝您的合作！
ABC公司 謹上

Unit 1

Unit 2

Unit 3

Unit 4

Unit 5

Unit 6

Unit 7

抄來抄去都抄這些！關鍵單字　　　⊗ ▢ ⊖

❶ term [tɝm] **n.** 條件，條款

❷ instruct [ɪn`strʌkt] **v.** 指示

❸ commercial [kə`mɝ.ʃəl] **adj.** 商業的

❹ credit [`krɛdɪt] **n.** 信用，賒購

❺ execute [`ɛksɪ.kjut] **v.** 執行

文法重點解析

解析重點 1

irrevocable L/C

L/C是信用狀letter of credit的縮寫形式,信用狀為國際貿易中最主要、最常見的付款方式。irrevocable L/C即「不可撤銷的信用狀」,是指開狀銀行一經開出,在有效期限內未經受益人或議付行等有關當事人同意,不得隨意修改或撤銷的信用狀。它的特徵是有開狀銀行確定的付款承諾和不可撤銷性。

解析重點 2

valid until Sep. 20

valid until...的意思是「有效期限至……」。這裡的valid指的是「有效的」,尤其指「有法律效力的」。舉例來說:

▶ You can't use this coupon. It's no longer valid.
你不能用這張折價券。已經沒有效用了。

▶ Your password is not valid. Please enter it again.
你的密碼無效,請再次輸入。

抄來抄去都抄這些！
補充例句

Unit
1

Unit
2

Unit
3

Unit
4

Unit
5

Unit
6

Unit
7

以下還有一些「申請信用狀」常用的例句供
參考，也可以活用在你的英文e-mail中喔！
別忘了，時間、人名等等的地方要換成符合
自己狀況的單字或句子。

❶ Thank you for your letter on March 6th
detailing your terms.
感謝您三月六日有關條款詳細情況的來信。

❷ This credit shall remain in force until
August 15th, 2020.
本狀到2020年8月15日止有效。

❸ We have instructed the bank you work
with to open a credit for US$ 20,000.
我方已經指示您的合作銀行開立金額為2
萬美元的信用狀。

❹ We hereby undertake to honor all drafts
drawn in accordance with the terms of
this credit.
所有按照本條款開具的匯票，我行保證兌付。

❺ All documents in English must be sent to
our bank in one lot.
所有英文單據須一次寄交我行。

❻ Please let us know when the order has
been executed.
當訂單已執行，請通知我們。

⊗ ▣ ⊖

From betty@mail.com
To miller@mail.com
Subject Application for Further Studies Abroad

Dear Mr. Miller,

My name is Betty Li and, as you already know, I am the supervisor [1] of the Research and Development [2] Department. I have been a loyal [3] employee of this company for ten years, and <u>plan to</u> remain so for many years to come.

However, pursuing [4] further studies abroad has always been my dream, a dream that is about to come true as my application [5] to the MBA program in an American university has just been accepted. I love our company and <u>would hate to</u> leave, which is why I am writing to ask, if possible, whether I will be able to keep my position [6] here after I finish my studies two years later.

Hoping for your support!

Sincerely Yours,
Betty Li

打開光碟，複製貼上，
不用一分鐘，抄完一封信！

★套色的部分為關鍵單字，在右頁可以看到解釋喔！
★劃底線的部分都有相關的文法補充，請翻到下一頁就可以看到囉！

中文翻譯

Unit
1

Unit
2

Unit
3

Unit
4

Unit
5

Unit
6

Unit
7

親愛的米樂先生：

我是貝蒂·李，如您所知，我是研發部的主管。我已在此公司忠誠地工作了十年，也希望未來多年能夠持續如此。

然而，我一直夢想著能夠出國進修，而這個夢想即將成真，因為我申請到一所美國大學讀MBA，學校剛剛接受我了。我熱愛公司，不希望離開，因此想寫信問您若可以的話，我兩年後進修完是否還能夠回來擔任相同的職位呢？

渴望能得到您的支持！

誠摯地，
貝蒂·李

抄來抄去都抄這些！關鍵單字　　　　⊗ ▢ ⊖

❶ supervisor [ˌsupəˋvaɪzə] **n.** 主管

❷ development [dɪˋvɛləpmənt] **n.** 發展

❸ loyal [ˋlɔɪəl] **adj.** 忠誠的

❹ pursue [pəˋsu] **v.** 追求

❺ application [ˌæpləˋkeʃən] **n.** 申請

❻ position [pəˋzɪʃən] **n.** 位置，職位

文法重點解析

解析重點**1**
plan to

這個片語表示「計畫要……」的意思。用在這封信中，意思是「我一直都是公司的忠誠員工，未來也計畫一直都是」。此處巧妙地利用plan to這個片語，言下之意就是：「我計畫要一直當個忠誠的好員工，這是『我的』計畫。如果您不願意接受讓我出國進修，打亂了這個計畫，那是您的決定，可不是我自己主動想要離開公司的喔！我自己可是計畫要一直待下來的啊！」是個若無其事撇清責任、把決定權交給對方的說法。小小的片語裡面也能包含很大的玄機呢。

解析重點**2**
would hate to

這個片語的意思是「我實在不想要……」的意思，背後包含了「我實在不想要，所以如果非得這麼做的話，那就是有人逼我」的含意。信中此處使用「would hate to leave」，言下之意就是：「我實在不想離開公司，但如果您不接受讓我出國進修，那我就不得不離開了。這是您決定的喔！不是我自己想要離開的！」再度巧妙地把責任丟給了對方。再看一些would hate to的例句：

▶I would hate to cause any problems.
　我可是不想要造成任何問題。

▶I would hate to be the one to tell him the bad news. 我可不想當跟他報告壞消息的人。

抄來抄去都抄這些！
補充例句

Unit 1

Unit 2

Unit 3

Unit 4

Unit 5

Unit 6

Unit 7

以下還有一些「申請出國進修」常用的例句供參考，也可以活用在你的英文e-mail中喔！別忘了，時間、人名等等的地方要換成符合自己狀況的單字或句子。

❶ You've always told us that you encourage employees to pursue further studies.
您總是告訴我們，您鼓勵員工持續進修。

❷ I will use all I've learned to make our company even better.
我會用我的所學讓公司變得更好。

❸ What I will learn will definitely contribute to our company's prosperous future.
我的所學肯定能夠對我們公司未來的繁榮有很大的貢獻。

❹ I will learn more about cutting-edge technology there.
我會在那裡學到更多最新的科技。

❺ This is to improve my professional skills and help me offer better services to the company.
這是要增進我的職業技術，並幫助我提供公司更好的服務。

❻ I have always been loyal to our company and promise to remain so.
我對我們公司一直很忠誠，也保證會一直維持如此。

抄來抄去都抄這些！

Unit 3 道謝與
道歉篇

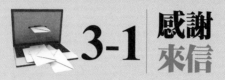

3-1 | 感謝來信

From ollie@mail.com
To alan@mail.com
Subject Thanks for your E-mail!

Dear Alan,

I was so delighted [1] to receive your letter. It has been a couple of years since we last talked, and I'm absolutely [2] flattered [3] that you remembered me and wrote to say hello.

Anyway, how's it going? We really need to catch up, but it's difficult because of the time difference. Well, at least we can still E-mail each other! I'm on my office computer right now, but when I get back home I'll <u>flood you with pics</u> of my new house.

Let's stay in touch! Bye for now.

Best Wishes,
Ollie

打開光碟，複製貼上，
不用一分鐘，抄完一封信！

★套色的部分為關鍵單字，在右頁可以看到解釋喔！
★劃底線的部分都有相關的文法補充，請翻到下一頁就可以看到囉！

中文翻譯

Unit
1

Unit
2

Unit
3

Unit
4

Unit
5

Unit
6

Unit
7

親愛的亞倫：

收到你的信，我真是太開心了。自從上次我們聊天以來已經好幾年了，你居然還記得我、寫信給我打招呼，我真是受寵若驚。

總之，最近如何？我們真的該好好聊聊了，但因為時差的關係很難。不過，至少我們還是可以寫電子郵件啊！我現在用的是公司的電腦，等我到家，我一定寄一堆我新家的照片給你。

保持聯絡喔！拜拜！

誠摯地，
歐麗

抄來抄去都抄這些！關鍵單字　　　　　　⊗ ⊡ ⊝

❶ delighted [dɪ`laɪtɪd] **adj.** 開心的
❷ absolutely [`æbsə͵lutlɪ] **adv.** 絕對地
❸ flattered [`flætəd] **adj.** 受寵若驚的

107

文法重點解析

catch up

catch up這個片語有「趕上」的意思，例如A跑在B前面，B好不容易追上了A，就可以說是「catch up」。但這封信中兩人又不跑步，為什麼用catch up這個片語呢？原來，這個片語也可以用來表示很久不見的兩人，因為一段時間都沒有對方的消息，必須在短短的時間內迅速「趕進度」，補足對方這一陣子以來發生的事。既然要在短時間內講很多事，不是也很有「趕上」的感覺嗎？因此就可以用catch up這個片語。

flood sb. with sth.

flood是水災的意思，此處用這個片語，就是要警告對方：「我待會會給你我新家的照片，而且會給你很多喔！多到像水災一樣把你淹沒喔！」好讓對方先有個心理準備。當然沒人會希望被多如水災的照片給淹沒，此處是個帶點負面的開玩笑說法，可以用在朋友之間，但在正式的信件中就別使用它比較好。

抄來抄去都抄這些！
補充例句

Unit
1

Unit
2

Unit
3

Unit
4

Unit
5

Unit
6

Unit
7

以下還有一些「感謝來信」常用的例句供參考，也可以活用在你的英文e-mail中喔！別忘了，時間、人名等等的地方要換成符合自己狀況的單字或句子。

1 I was excited to get your letter.
我很興奮能夠收到你的來信。

2 Thank you for thinking of me.
謝謝你想到我。

3 I really should have written you sooner.
我真應該早點寫信給你的。

4 It's been some time since I last written you an E-mail.
我已經有一陣子沒寫E-mail給你了。

5 How have you been these days?
你這些天過得如何？

6 We need to meet up and have a good chat.
我們一定要見個面好好聊聊。

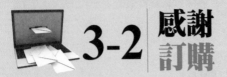

3-2 感謝訂購

From minisoft@mail.com
To kane@mail.com
Subject Thanks for your Order

Dear Mr. Kane,

Thank you very much for ordering [1] our software [2], Mini Diary.

Your purchase [3] information is attached. We will ship the product to you <u>on receipt of</u> your payment [4].

If there are any other commodities [5] you are interested in, please <u>feel free to</u> contact us for further information.

Sincerely Yours,
Minisoft Co.

打開光碟,複製貼上,
不用一分鐘,抄完一封信!

★套色的部分為關鍵單字,在右頁可以看到解釋喔!
★劃底線的部分都有相關的文法補充,請翻到下一頁就可以看到囉!

中文翻譯

Unit 1
Unit 2
Unit 3
Unit 4
Unit 5
Unit 6
Unit 7

親愛的凱恩先生：

感謝您訂購敝公司的「迷你日記」軟體。

訂購確認資料已經隨函附上，在確認收到您的付款後，商品將會寄出。

如果您對敝公司的其他產品有興趣，並需要進一步的資訊，請不吝諮詢。

迷你軟體公司 謹上

抄來抄去都抄這些！關鍵單字 ⊗ ▢ ⊖

❶ order [`ɔrdə] v. 訂購
❷ software [`sɔft͵wɛr] n. 軟體
❸ purchase [`pɜtʃəs] v./n. 購買
❹ payment [`pemənt] n. 付款
❺ commodity [kə`mɑdətɪ] n. 商品

文法重點解析

解析重點1

on receipt of

receipt是receive的名詞版，意思是「收到」或
「接收」。on receipt of的意思是「在收到後馬
上……」，on表達的是「一（發生某事），立
刻就會（發生另一件事）」的意思。因此，此處
整句的意思就是「一收到您的付款，就會立即出
貨」，也就是說「付款」這件事發生後，「出
貨」這件事就會立刻發生。言下之意就是暗示對
方：「如果您不付款，我們就不會出貨」，也就
是要請對方趕快付款囉！

解析重點2

feel free to

這個片語的意思是「隨意地……」、「可以隨意
（做某事）也沒關係」，此處就是表示「可以隨
意來跟我們索取資訊也沒關係」的意思。再舉幾
個使用的例子：

▶ If you have any questions, feel free to ask.
   如果你有問題，那就隨意問吧。

▶ Feel free to take some cookies on the plate.
   隨意拿一些盤子上的餅乾吧。

抄來抄去都抄這些！
補充例句

Unit 1
Unit 2
Unit 3
Unit 4
Unit 5
Unit 6
Unit 7

以下還有一些「感謝訂購」常用的例句供參考，也可以活用在你的英文e-mail中喔！別忘了，時間、人名等等的地方要換成符合自己狀況的單字或句子。

① Thank you very much for ordering our textiles.
非常感謝您訂購我們的紡織品。

② The purchase confirmation has been attached.
訂購確認書已經隨函附上了。

③ Thank you for your interest in our software.
感謝您對我們的軟體感興趣。

④ Please contact us directly for our product catalogue.
想要我們的產品目錄的話，請直接與我們聯絡。

⑤ Your order will be shipped in a maximum of 2 working days.
您的訂單將會在兩個工作天內出貨。

⑥ Please don't hesitate to ask if you have questions regarding the product.
如果對於該產品有任何疑問請不用猶豫，可以問我們。

113

3-3 感謝
關照、款待

From ken@mail.com
To mary@mail.com
Subject Thanks for your Kindness and Hospitality

Dear Mary,

I would like to thank you for your enthusiasm [1] and hospitality [2] during my visit to your country. It was my first time staying overseas [3] for two months, so I was a little nervous in the beginning. However, you treated me like a member of your own family and made me feel very much at home. I am very grateful.

I hope one day you'll have a chance to visit my country as well. I'll definitely try to be the best host [4] possible!

Kindest Regards,
Ken

打開光碟，複製貼上，
不用一分鐘，抄完一封信！

★套色的部分為關鍵單字，在右頁可以看到解釋喔！
★劃底線的部分都有相關的文法補充，請翻到下一頁就可以看到囉！

中文翻譯

Unit
1

Unit
2

Unit
3

Unit
4

Unit
5

Unit
6

Unit
7

親愛的瑪麗：

我想感謝您在我拜訪您的國家時，給了我很多的熱情與照顧。這是我第一次在國外住兩個月，所以我一開始有點緊張。然而，您待我就像家人一樣，而且讓我感覺彷彿回到家一樣。我非常感激。

我希望有一天您也有機會拜訪我的國家。我一定會試著成為最好的主人！

誠摯地，
肯恩

抄來抄去都抄這些！關鍵單字　　　　　　　⊗ ▢ ⊖

❶ enthusiasm [ɪn`θjuzɪˌæzəm] **n.** 熱情
❷ hospitality [ˌhɑspɪ`tælətɪ] **n.** 好客，殷勤
❸ overseas [`ovɚ`siz] **adv.** 海外地
❹ host [host] **n.** 主人

文法重點解析

解析重點 **1**

treat sb. like

treat當作動詞時,意思是「對待」,而片語
「treat sb./sth. like...」就是「把(某人或某事)
當作(某人或某事)來對待」。看看幾個例句,
就能明白它的用法:

▶ The old lady treats her cat like her own daughter.
這個老太太把貓當作女兒一樣對待。

▶ He always treats other people like dirt.
他總是把其他人當作糞土一樣對待。

解析重點 **2**

feel at home

片語「feel at home」的意思就是「感覺彷彿回到
家一般」,此處加上very much強調語氣,表示
「感覺超級像回到家一般」。注意very much只能
加在at home的前面,要是變成「very much feel
at home」、「feel at home very much」都不對
喔!

抄來抄去都抄這些！
補充例句

Unit 1

Unit 2

Unit 3

Unit 4

Unit 5

Unit 6

Unit 7

以下還有一些「感謝關照、款待」常用的例句供參考，也可以活用在你的英文e-mail中喔！別忘了，時間、人名等等的地方要換成符合自己狀況的單字或句子。

❶ Thank you very much for your warm hospitality during my stay.
非常感謝您在我逗留期間熱情款待。

❶ Thank you for your kindness.
謝謝你的善意。

❷ Please give my sincere regards to your family.
請代我向您的家人致上誠摯的問候。

❸ I am extremely grateful for what you did for me.
我非常感激你為我做的一切。

❹ I can never thank you enough for your hospitality.
對於您的熱情款待，我再怎麼謝也謝不完。

❺ Yours is the best home-stay family one could ask for.
你們家真是最棒的寄宿家庭。

3-4 感謝介紹客戶

From eastjustice@mail.com
To burns@mail.com
Subject Thanks for the Introduction

Dear Mr. Burns,

Thank you for introducing [1] us to E-Trade USA. We met with Mr. Tom Johnson, their Executive [2] Director [3], in Shanghai this week and discussed their legal [4] needs in China. Mr. Johnson holds you in high regard and is particularly [5] interested in several of our attorneys [6] educated and trained in the U.S. We look forward to providing E-Trade with the finest and most cost-effective services.

We owe you the greatest debt [7] of gratitude [8].

Sincerely Yours,
East Justice Law Firm

打開光碟，複製貼上，
不用一分鐘，抄完一封信！

★套色的部分為關鍵單字，在右頁可以看到解釋喔！
★劃底線的部分都有相關的文法補充，請翻到下一頁就可以看到囉！

中文翻譯

親愛的伯恩斯先生：

謝謝您介紹我們給美國電子貿易公司。我們這週與他們的執行董事湯姆‧強森在上海見過面，討論了他們在中國的法律需求。強森先生非常尊敬您，對於我們在美國受教育與培訓的幾位律師特別感興趣。我們相當期待能夠提供美國電子貿易公司最優質、價格也最合理的服務。

我們由衷地感謝您。

誠摯地，
東方正義律師事務所

Unit 1

Unit 2

Unit 3

Unit 4

Unit 5

Unit 6

Unit 7

抄來抄去都抄這些！關鍵單字

❶ introduce [ˌɪntrə`djus] **v.** 介紹

❷ executive [ɪg`zɛkjʊtɪv] **adj.** 執行的，行政的

❸ director [də`rɛktə] **n.** 主管，主任

❹ legal [`ligl] **adj.** 合法的，法律的

❺ particularly [pə`tɪkjələ·lɪ] **adv.** 特定地，特別地

❻ attorney [ə`tɝnɪ] **n.** 律師

❼ debt [dɛt] **n.** 債務

❽ gratitude [`grætəˌtjud] **n.** 感激

文法重點解析

解析重點1
holds you in high regard

hold sb. in high regard的意思是「非常看重、敬重某人」。regard有「認為」、「看法」的意思，對某人的「看法」很「高」，可想而知就是非常敬重他啦！這裡使用這一句除了順口稱讚對方讓對方開心以外，也順便傳達了「就是因為強森先生這麼敬重你，我們才能跟他談得這麼順利」，進一步再次拐個彎表達對對方的感謝之情。

解析重點2
cost-effective

cost-effective字面上看起來像是「價格很有效」。價格很有效是什麼意思呢？其實就是指「花少少的價格，得到大大的效益」啦！使用在此處就表示承諾會提供E-Trade公司「不貴但效益很高」的服務。相反地，如果你在職場上覺得別人提出來的方法投資報酬率不高，就算投入很多錢也不見得會有效，就可以反過來說他的想法「not cost-effective」。

抄來抄去都抄這些！
補充例句

Unit
1

Unit
2

Unit
3

Unit
4

Unit
5

Unit
6

Unit
7

以下還有一些「感謝介紹客戶」常用的例
句供參考，也可以活用在你的英文e-mail中
喔！別忘了，時間、人名等等的地方要換成
符合自己狀況的單字或句子。

❶ Thank you so much for introducing ABC
Co. to us.
非常感謝您介紹ABC公司給我們。

❷ I am pleased to say it looks like we will
build a new relationship with them.
我很開心地要通知您，看來我們將會和他
們建立新的關係。

❸ Again, we appreciate your continued
support.
再次感謝您一直以來的支持。

❹ Thank you for the confidence you have
shown in us.
感謝您對我們充滿信心。

❺ We really owe you for helping us establish
this relationship.
我們很感謝您幫助我們建立這個關係。

❻ We owe you big time.
你們真是幫了我們超大的一個忙。

3-5 感謝協助

⊗ ▣ ⚊

From browns@mail.com
To whites@mail.com
Subject Thanks for the Help

Dear Mr. and Mrs. White,

We are writing to thank you for helping us move in last week. Sorry it took us so long to send this E-mail—we got our wi-fi set up just yesterday!

To thank you for your kind assistance [1], we would love to invite your whole family over to our (freshly [2] decorated [3]) place for dinner. We don't have a set date yet, but when we do decide, we'll be sure to let you know!

Sincerely Yours,
Mark and Emily Brown

打開光碟，複製貼上，
不用一分鐘，抄完一封信！

★套色的部分為關鍵單字，在右頁可以看到解釋喔！
★劃底線的部分都有相關的文法補充，請翻到下一頁就可以看到囉！

中文翻譯

親愛的懷特先生與太太：

我們寫信來是要感謝您上週幫我們搬進新家。很抱歉花了我們這麼久寄這封E-mail，我們昨天才把無線網路架設好的！

為了感謝您善意的幫助，我們希望能邀請您全家到我們（剛裝潢好的）家吃晚餐。我們還沒有一個確定的日期，但等到決定好了，我們肯定會通知您的！

誠摯地，

馬克與愛密麗·布朗

Unit
1

Unit
2

Unit
3

Unit
4

Unit
5

Unit
6

Unit
7

抄來抄去都抄這些！關鍵單字　✕◻◻

❶ assistance [əˋsɪstəns] **n.** 協助

❷ freshly [ˋfrɛʃlɪ] **adv.** 新鮮地，新近地

❸ decorate [ˋdɛkəˏret] **v.** 裝飾，裝潢

文法重點解析

set date

set可以當作動詞和形容詞。當動詞時,有「放置、擺設」的意思;而當作形容詞時,有「已經決定好的、確定不變的」的意思,因此set date的意思就是「已經確定(而且不太會改變)的日期」。信中此處使用這個片語即是表示雖然決定了要請對方一家吃飯,但日期還沒有確定。

be sure to

片語「be sure to」的意思是「肯定會……」,帶有保證的語氣。來看幾個例子:

▶ If I hear any news about him, I'll be sure to tell you about it.

如果我聽到任何和他有關的消息,我肯定會告訴你。

▶ She's sure to go mad when she learns about this.

她聽到這件事肯定會發飆。

▶ We'll be sure to give you a call later.

待會我們肯定會打個電話給你。

抄來抄去都抄這些！
補充例句

Unit
1

Unit
2

Unit
3

Unit
4

Unit
5

Unit
6

Unit
7

以下還有一些「感謝協助」常用的例句供參考，也可以活用在你的英文e-mail中喔！別忘了，時間、人名等等的地方要換成符合自己狀況的單字或句子。

❶ Thank you for all your kindness and support.
非常感謝您的友好和支持。

❷ I am writing this to express my thanks to all of you.
此信是為了表達對各位的感激之情。

❸ We are lucky to have friends like you.
能有你們這樣的朋友，我們很幸運。

❹ We are extremely grateful for your assistance.
我們非常感激您的協助。

❺ Thank you for giving us a hand when we needed it the most.
謝謝你們在我們最需要的時候伸出援手。

❻ Thanks for offering to help.
謝謝你們自願提供幫忙。

3-6 感謝
合作

From ct@mail.com
To wells@mail.com
Subject Thanks for Working with Us

Dear Mr. Wells,

This is to express great gratitude [1] for your close collaboration [2] with us.

We have had a profitable [3] year working with you. In fact, we had so much success that we are already considering expanding [4] our business, and we are endlessly [5] grateful towards you for that! We do hope that we continue to collaborate in the future, and expect it to be a win-win situation [6] for both us and you.

Yours Truly,
CT Corporation

打開光碟,複製貼上,
不用一分鐘,抄完一封信!

★套色的部分**為關鍵單字,在右頁可以看到解釋喔!**
★劃底線的部分**都有相關的文法補充,請翻到下一頁就可以看到囉!**

中文翻譯

Unit 1

Unit 2

Unit 3

Unit 4

Unit 5

Unit 6

Unit 7

親愛的威爾斯先生：

這封信是想強烈感激您與我們密切的合作。

我們與您合作的一年來獲得相當多的利益。事實上，我們成功得已經開始考慮擴展事業，而為此我們對您真是感激不盡！我們希望未來能夠持續合作，也預期這對我們與您都是雙贏的情況。

誠摯地，

CT公司

抄來抄去都抄這些！關鍵單字　⊗ ☐ ⊖

1 gratitude [`grætə,tjud] n. 感謝

2 collaboration [kə,læbə`reʃən] n. 合作

3 profitable [`prɑfɪtəbl] adj. 有利益的

4 expand [ɪk`spænd] v. 擴張，擴展

5 endlessly [`ɛndləslɪ] adv. 無止境地

6 situation [,sɪtʃʊ`eʃən] n. 處境，狀況

127

文法重點解析

解析重點 1

collaboration

說到「合作」，大家可能常會想到cooperation這個單字。沒錯，這個單字和collaboration一樣都是「合作」的意思，但兩者之間有一些差別喔！cooperation比較被動，帶點「配合」的味道，例如若有人拿著槍叫你把錢都交出來，而你很「合作」地把錢交出去了，這就是cooperation；或若你的老闆希望員工「合作」一點，固定每週將辦公室打掃一次，這也是cooperation。

collaboration表達的則比較積極一些，指的是雙方（或多方）共同對於某事付出貢獻、一起做某件事、完成某件事。舉例來說，若你找到一個吉他手、一個貝斯手、一個鼓手和一個主唱，一群人一起表演了一首歌，這就是collaboration囉！

解析重點 2

endlessly

endlessly是「無止盡地」的意思，舉幾個例子來說：

▶ He talks endlessly if no one stops him.
　如果沒人阻止，他可以無止盡地一直講下去。

▶ She complains endlessly about her husband.
　她無止盡地一直抱怨她丈夫的事。

而在信中此處，使用endlessly是表示「感謝得無止盡」的意思，也就是我們中文常說的「感激不盡」。

抄來抄去都抄這些！
補充例句

Unit
1

Unit
2

Unit
3

Unit
4

Unit
5

Unit
6

Unit
7

以下還有一些「感謝合作」常用的例句供參考，也可以活用在你的英文e-mail中喔！別忘了，時間、人名等等的地方要換成符合自己狀況的單字或句子。

❶ It was a pleasure to work with you.
與您一起工作是很開心的事。

❷ Please convey my thanks to all the staff of your company.
請代我向貴公司所有員工轉達感激之意。

❸ I hope that we can continue to collaborate in future projects.
希望在未來的專案中還能持續合作。

❹ I would like to continue working with you for many years to come.
我希望可以繼續和你們合作很多年。

❺ Thank you for your cooperation during this year.
謝謝你們這一年來的配合。

❻ I believe that our collaboration works well for both sides.
我覺得我們的合作對兩邊都很有幫助。

129

⊗▣⊖

From lfco@mail.com
To brown@mail.com
Subject Apology for Faulty Products

Dear Mr. Brown,

We are very sorry to hear that you found defective [1] goods in our shipment [2].

We will certainly accept the return of these items and send you replacements [3] at once. Please accept our apologies [4] for any inconvenience [5] this may have caused you. I assure you that I have instructed the quality [6] control manager to make certain this does not happen again.

Yours Truly,
LF Corporation

打開光碟，複製貼上，
不用一分鐘，抄完一封信！

★套色的部分為關鍵單字，在右頁可以看到解釋喔！
★劃底線的部分都有相關的文法補充，請翻到下一頁就可以看到囉！

中文翻譯

Unit
1

Unit
2

Unit
3

Unit
4

Unit
5

Unit
6

Unit
7

親愛的布朗先生：
對於運往貴公司的貨物中出現了瑕疵品，我們感到十分抱歉。

我們當然會接受退貨，新的貨品也會立即寄出。對於可能給您帶來的不便，請接受我們真誠的道歉。我向您保證，今後在品管人員的認真檢查下，不會再發生此類的事情。

誠摯地，
LF公司

抄來抄去都抄這些！關鍵單字　　　　　⊗◻⊖

① defective [dɪˋfɛktɪv] **adj.** 有瑕疵的
② shipment [ˋʃɪpmənt] **n.** 貨物
③ replacement [rɪˋplesmənt] **n.** 替代品
④ apology [əˋpɑlədʒɪ] **n.** 道歉
⑤ inconvenience [ˏɪnkənˋvinjəns] **n.** 不便
⑥ quality [ˋkwɑlətɪ] **n.** 品質

文法重點解析

解析重點 **1**

I assure you

「I assure you...」這個句型是「我向您保證……」的意思，用在此處就是要藉由這個充滿了「擔保」、「保證」、「安撫」意味的單字，讓對方感到安心，覺得同樣的錯誤不會再犯第二次。再來看看幾個例句：

▶ I assure you that I will never make the same mistake again.

我向您保證，我再也不會犯同樣的錯了。

▶ I assure you that I have never cheated on you and never will.

我向你保證，我從來沒有腳踏兩條船，以後也絕對不會。

解析重點 **2**

instruct

instruct這個字有「指示」的意思，像是你的同事教你怎麼一個步驟一個步驟使用影印機，這個動作就是instruct；你的老師要你一步一步填完單子，也是instruct。用在這封信中，說會「指示」品管人員認真檢查，其實也是指出「是品管人員沒有認真檢查喔！不是我喔！從此以後我會『指示』他認真檢查喔！」不但若無其事地表達了錯不在自己，還順便表示若品管人員以後認真檢查，那自己也有功勞（因為是他「指示」品管人員去檢查的），真是個充滿心機的作法啊。

抄來抄去都抄這些！
補充例句

Unit 1

Unit 2

Unit 3

Unit 4

Unit 5

Unit 6

Unit 7

以下還有一些「為瑕疵品道歉」常用的例句供參考，也可以活用在你的英文e-mail中喔！別忘了，時間、人名等等的地方要換成符合自己狀況的單字或句子。

❶ I am sorry to hear that you have received defective goods.

很抱歉聽說您收到了有瑕疵的貨物。

❷ We will, of course, accept the return of these items.

我們當然會接受退貨。

❸ I apologize for all the trouble caused.

對於造成的不便，我很抱歉。

❹ Please accept my apology for any inconvenience my mistake has caused you.

由於我的失誤給您造成的不便，請接受我的道歉。

❺ I do apologize for the problems you found in the products.

對於您在貨品中發現的問題，我感到很抱歉。

❻ We will send a replacement within this week.

我們會在這禮拜內送出替代品。

3-8 為交貨延遲道歉

From plastic@mail.com
To steele@mail.com
Subject Apology for Delayed Delivery

Dear Mr. Steele,

Please accept our profound [1] apologies for the late delivery of goods to your company.

The delay [2] was due to a mix-up at our freight company, and we will make sure we work with those who can ensure [3] that all delivery deadlines [4] are met in the future.

We hope that you will forgive us for our unintentional [5] mistake and continue to purchase items from us.

Yours Truly,
Plastic Co.

打開光碟,複製貼上,
不用一分鐘,抄一封信!

★套色的部分為關鍵單字,在右頁可以看到解釋喔!
★劃底線的部分都有相關的文法補充,請翻到下一頁就可以看到囉!

中文翻譯

Unit 1

Unit 2

Unit 3

Unit 4

Unit 5

Unit 6

Unit 7

親愛的史帝爾先生：
對於延遲寄送貴公司貨品一事，請接受我們深深的道歉。

此次延遲是由於運輸公司出現了紕漏。今後我們一定會與能夠守時的運輸公司合作。

希望您能原諒我們無心的錯誤，並繼續購買我們的產品。

誠摯地，
塑膠公司

抄來抄去都抄這些！關鍵單字　　　　　⊗□⊖

❶ profound [prə`faʊnd] adj. 深奧的，深切的

❷ delay [dɪ`le] n. 耽擱

❸ ensure [ɪn`ʃʊr] v. 確保，保證

❹ deadline [`dɛd͵laɪn] n. 最後期限，截止時間

❺ unintentional [͵ʌnɪn`tɛnʃənl] adj.
　無心的，無意的

文法重點解析

解析重點**1**

mix-up

片語「mix up」是把兩種以上的東西「混合」在一起的意思。那麼如果把事情混合在一起會怎樣呢？那就很容易「搞混」、「混亂」了，因此名詞「mix-up」就可以表達「搞混的事」、「混亂」的意思。此處使用這個字就是想表達之所以交貨延遲，是因為「搞混了」，不是「故意」延遲的，藉以強調這只是一次單純無意的失誤，不會再發生，讓對方感到安心一些。

解析重點**2**

meet a deadline

meet有「遇見」、「見面」的意思。那為什麼要和deadline（最後繳交期限）「見面」呢？原來meet a deadline就是「在最後繳交期限之前順利繳交」、「在最後期限之前順利做完」的意思。信中的句子「we will make sure we work with those who can ensure that all delivery deadlines are met in the future」即是「我們今後只會和能準時交件的廠商合作」，若無其事地就將錯推到了廠商頭上，是個帶點小心機的作法。

抄來抄去都抄這些！
補充例句

Unit
1

Unit
2

Unit
3

Unit
4

Unit
5

Unit
6

Unit
7

以下還有一些「為交貨延遲道歉」常用的例
句供參考，也可以活用在你的英文e-mail中
喔！別忘了，時間、人名等等的地方要換成
符合自己狀況的單字或句子。

❶ I am sorry to hear that you received your
order late.
聽說您很晚才收到貨物，我非常抱歉。

❷ We will work with reliable freight
companies in the future.
我們未來會與可靠的運輸公司工作。

❸ I apologize for the inconvenience caused
by the late delivery of goods.
對於延遲交貨給您帶來的不便我感到很抱
歉。

❹ Please accept my apology for our
carelessness during the shipment.
為我們運輸中的疏忽向您致上真誠的道歉。

❺ I do apologize for the late delivery of your
products.
對於延遲運輸您的貨品，我感到很抱歉。

❻ We will compensate for all losses caused
by this late delivery.
對於此次延遲出貨造成的所有損
失，我們會全權負責。

3-9 為延遲付款道歉

From cecily@mail.com
To white@mail.com
Subject Apology for Delayed Remittance

Dear Mr. White,

We are terribly sorry for the late remittance [1].
As the wines are not yet sold, nor are they
likely to be for some time, we were unable to
pay you back in time. Please accept our most
earnest [2] apology. We have already gotten our
financial problems sorted out and are quite
certain that something like this will not ever
happen again.

We promise that you will receive the remittance
on time in the future, and appreciate [3] your
understanding [4].

Yours Faithfully,
Cecily Jones

打開光碟,複製貼上,
不用一分鐘,抄完一封信!

★套色的部分為關鍵單字,在右頁可以看到解釋喔!
★劃底線的部分都有相關的文法補充,請翻到下一頁就可以看到囉!

中文翻譯

Unit 1

Unit 2

Unit 3

Unit 4

Unit 5

Unit 6

Unit 7

親愛的懷特先生：

非常抱歉這次逾期匯款了。由於葡萄酒尚未售出，近期也難有改觀，我們才無法及時付款。請接受我們誠摯的歉意。我們已經解決所有財務方面的問題了，同時我們也很確定這樣的事情絕對不會再發生了。

我們保證以後一定會準時匯款，並非常感謝您的諒解。

誠摯地，
希斯麗·瓊斯

抄來抄去都抄這些！關鍵單字　　　　⊗ ☐ ⊖

❶ remittance [rɪ`mɪtns] **n.** 匯款

❷ earnest [`ɝnɪst] **adj.** 誠摯的

❸ appreciate [ə`priʃɪ‚et] **v.** 感謝，欣賞

❹ understanding [‚ʌndɚ`stændɪŋ] **n.** 理解

文法重點解析

解析重點 1

on time

on time的意思是「準時」。這封信前面一段還出現了一個長得很像的in time，這兩者之間有什麼差別呢？原來，in time指的是「趕在最後期限內」，也就是說如果最後期限是10點，那無論是9點完成、9點半完成、9點59分完成，都算是「in time」。on time則是「準時」的意思，也就是說如果最後期限是10點，而剛好在10點完成，就叫做「on time」。

解析重點 2

understanding

大家應該常常會聽到一句：「Do you understand?」（你懂嗎？）問的可能是你有沒有聽懂某事、或是否理解某個情形。而與understand相關的名詞understanding也一樣，可以表達「理解」的意思，在這封信中「appreciate your understanding」就表示「感謝您的理解」。其實這也是個技巧性的作法，因為對方根本就還沒有理解，說不定對方正因為沒收到款項而生氣呢！然而信中還是擅自感謝了對方的理解，這樣對方就會覺得既然人家都已經謝了，好像不理解也不行了……是很好用的一招喔！

抄來抄去都抄這些！

補充例句

Unit
1

Unit
2

Unit
3

Unit
4

Unit
5

Unit
6

Unit
7

以下還有一些「為延遲付款道歉」常用的例句供參考，也可以活用在你的英文e-mail中喔！別忘了，時間、人名等等的地方要換成符合自己狀況的單字或句子。

❶ Please accept our sincere apology for any trouble it may cause.
對於可能因此給您造成的麻煩，請接受我們真誠的道歉。

❷ We are very sorry for sending in the payment so late.
我們很抱歉這麼晚才付款。

❸ I promise that this will not happen again in the future.
我保證未來不會再發生了。

❹ Thank you very much for your understanding.
非常感謝您的理解。

❺ We are sure that such a delay will never happen again.
我們很確定，這樣的延遲永遠不會再發生了。

❻ We will make sure to be extra careful to be on time in the future.
我們未來一定會特別小心準時。

3-10 | 為延遲回覆道歉

⊗◻⊖

From eric@mail.com
To keller@mail.com
Subject Apology for Late Reply

Dear Mr. Keller,

Please excuse me for getting back to you so late.

I have been swamped with work and was unable [1] to check my mailbox [2] until now. I am very sorry about that. I was shocked to see all those E-mails from you, and felt so terrible for not being able to reply to you earlier.

I will be glad to accept your proposal [3] and look forward to meeting you when you come to New York and discussing the related [4] details.

Best Regards,
Eric Daniels

打開光碟，複製貼上，
不用一分鐘，抄完一封信！

★套色的部分為**關鍵單字**，在右頁可以看到解釋喔！
★劃底線的部分都有相關的文法補充，請翻到下一頁就可以看到囉！

中文翻譯

Unit
1

Unit
2

Unit
3

Unit
4

Unit
5

Unit
6

Unit
7

親愛的凱勒先生：
請原諒我這麼晚才回覆您的郵件。

我工作非常地忙碌，直到現在才能夠檢查我的信箱。我為此感到非常抱歉。我看到您寄了那麼多封電子郵件非常驚訝，也覺得很抱歉沒有辦法早點回應您。

我很樂意接受您的提案，也很期待在您到紐約時與您見面、討論相關的細節。

誠摯地，
愛瑞克‧丹尼爾斯

抄來抄去都抄這些！關鍵單字　　　　　✕ □ ⊖

❶ unable [ʌn`ebl] adj. 沒辦法的，不能的
❷ mailbox [`mel͵bɑks] n. 信箱
❸ proposal [prə`pozl] n. 提案，提議
❹ related [rɪ`letɪd] adj. 相關的

文法重點解析

解析重點 1

get back to sb.

「get back to 某人」這個片語意思是「回覆某人」、「與某人聯絡並告知答覆」。再來看幾個例子：

▶ I don't know if I should accept. Let me think about it and I'll get back to you later.
我不知道該不該接受。讓我想一下，我過一會再回覆你。

▶ My boss says he will get back to you soon, so don't worry.
我老闆說他不久後會回覆你，所以不用擔心。

解析重點 2

be swamped with

swamp是「沼澤」的意思。一旦踏進了沼澤，很容易就陷入泥淖中無法脫身，這感覺是不是很像被大量的工作纏身而抽不開身呢？所以要描述事情太多，無法抽身時，就可以用be swamped with 這個片語。像是be swamped with work就是個非常常見的搭配用法，畢竟最可能讓人抽不開身的事就是工作啦。

抄來抄去都抄這些！

補充例句

Unit
1

Unit
2

Unit
3

Unit
4

Unit
5

Unit
6

Unit
7

以下還有一些「為延遲回覆道歉」常用的例句供參考，也可以活用在你的英文e-mail中喔！別忘了，時間、人名等等的地方要換成符合自己狀況的單字或句子。

❶ I'm terribly sorry for the late reply.
這麼晚回覆您，我真的很抱歉。

❷ I didn't realize that your E-mail had been sorted into the junk mail folder.
我沒發現您的電子郵件被分類到垃圾郵件夾去了。

❸ I saw your E-mail only just now.
我剛剛才看到您的電子郵件。

❹ I have been sick for a couple of weeks, which was why I couldn't check my mail.
我病了幾週，所以才沒辦法收信。

❺ I have been extremely busy these days.
我這一陣子很忙。

❻ My account got hacked, so I didn't realize I got an E-mail from you.
我的帳號被盜了，所以我才沒發現您有寄信給我。

3-11 為違約道歉

From shunda@mail.com
To norris@mail.com
Subject Apology for Unexpected Violation of Contract

Dear Mr. Norris,

We apologize for <u>failing to</u> deliver your goods at the scheduled [1] time in accordance [2] with the contract [3] we signed.

Unfortunately, owing to excessive [4] demand last month, we were unable to fill all orders on time. However, we will compensate [5] for all your economic [6] losses caused by the <u>unexpected</u> violation [7] of the contract.

Thank you very much for your understanding.

Sincerely Yours,
Shunda Co.

打開光碟，複製貼上，
不用一分鐘，抄完一封信！

★套色的部分為關鍵單字，在右頁可以看到解釋喔！
★劃底線的部分都有相關的文法補充，請翻到下一頁就可以看到囉！

中文翻譯

親愛的那瑞斯先生：
非常抱歉我們未能在簽訂的合約中預定的時間交貨。

不幸的是，由於上個月訂單過多，我們沒能按時交付所有的訂單。不過，由於此次意外違反合約，我們會賠償您所有的經濟損失。

非常感謝您的諒解。

誠摯地，
順達公司

Unit 1
Unit 2
Unit 3
Unit 4
Unit 5
Unit 6
Unit 7

抄來抄去都抄這些！關鍵單字　　　　　　　×□—

❶ schedule [`skɛdʒʊl] **v.** 訂定行程
❷ accordance [ə`kɔrdəns] **n.** 依據
❸ contract [kən`trækt] **n.** 合約
❹ excessive [ɪk`sɛsɪv] **adj.** 過多的
❺ compensate [`kampən‚set] **v.** 補償
❻ economic [‚ikə`namɪk] **adj.** 經濟的
❼ violation [‚vaɪə`leʃən] **n.** 違反，侵害

文法重點解析

解析重點 1
failing to

fail to這個片語的意思是「沒能做到（某事）」，
後面要接原形動詞喔！來看幾個例句：

▶ I fail to see why this is such a big deal.
　我實在沒辦法看出這件事到底有什麼重要。

▶ He failed to send the application letter on time.
　他沒能及時把申請信函送出去。

解析重點 2
unexpected

expected是「預期的」的意思，前面加上了表
示「沒有、無、不」的字首「un-」，意思變成
「預期之外的」、「意外的」。此處用了「the
unexpected violation of contract」這個句子，指
「意外違反合約」，隱含著「違反合約這件事我
們自己也很意外」的意思，目的是要告訴對方違
反合約這件事絕對不是常態，這一次是非常罕見
的意外事件，同時也讓對方安心，覺得以後應該
不會再發生。

抄來抄去都抄這些！
補充例句

Unit
1

Unit
2

Unit
3

Unit
4

Unit
5

Unit
6

Unit
7

以下還有一些「為違約道歉」常用的例句供
參考，也可以活用在你的英文e-mail中喔！
別忘了，時間、人名等等的地方要換成符合
自己狀況的單字或句子。

❶ I would like to apologize for the lengthy
delay in shipping your order.
我要為交貨延遲了這麼久向您道歉。

❷ We are doing everything to ensure that
your order will be shipped without further
delay.
我們會盡最大努力保證您訂購的貨物裝運
不會再有任何延誤。

❸ Please accept our sincere apology for our
violation of the contract.
對於我方違反合約的事，請接受我們真誠
的歉意。

❹ We will make certain that you will receive
your shipment by next Tuesday at the
latest.
我們保證最遲下週二您就會收到貨物。

❺ We promise that the shipment will arrive
within the week.
我們保證，貨物這週就會抵達。

×□—

抄來抄去都抄這些！

Unit **4** 通知篇

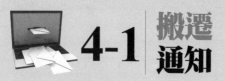

4-1 搬遷通知

From tony@mail.com
To all@mail.com
Subject We're Moving!

Dear Sirs,

We are pleased to announce that our Marketing [1] Department will be moving to Seaside [2] Mansion [3], Room 1704 at 36 Leo Street from July 8. Our telephone number remains unchanged [4] and mail should continue to be addressed to <u>P.O Box</u> No. 31.

Each staff member of our company <u>takes this opportunity to</u> solicit [5] your continued support.

Yours Faithfully,
Tony Hardy
Marketing Manager

打開光碟，複製貼上，
不用一分鐘，抄完一封信！

★套色的部分為關鍵單字，在右頁可以看到解釋喔！
★劃底線的部分都有相關的文法補充，請翻到下一頁就可以看到囉！

中文翻譯

Unit
1

Unit
2

Unit
3

Unit
4

Unit
5

Unit
6

Unit
7

親愛的顧客：

我們很高興地宣布，本公司行銷部門自7月8日起將遷往里歐街36號的海濱大廈1704室。我們的電話號碼保持不變，郵件地址仍為31號郵政信箱。

本公司全體人員藉此機會懇請各位繼續給予支持與關注。

誠摯地，
東尼・哈迪
行銷部門經理

抄來抄去都抄這些！關鍵單字　　　　⊗▢⊖

❶ marketing [`mɑrkɪtɪŋ] n. 行銷

❷ seaside [`si͵saɪd] n. 海邊的

❸ mansion [`mænʃən] n. 公寓，大廈，宅邸

❹ unchanged [ʌn`tʃendʒd] adj. 不變的

❺ solicit [sə`lɪsɪt] v. 懇求，請求

文法重點解析

解析重點1

P.O. Box

P.O. Box其實就是Post Office Box的縮寫，也就是郵局信箱啦！如果居住或工作的地方沒有一個自己的地址或可以投遞信件的管道，就可以在郵局申請一個專屬於你或者公司的信箱，只要信來時去郵局領就行了。當然這服務通常是要錢的。

解析重點2

take this opportunity to

opportunity是「機會」的意思，而片語「take this opportunity to」就是「藉此機會做某事」。來看幾個例句：

▶ She saw a movie star on the street and took this opportunity to ask for a signature.

她在街上看到了一個電影明星，便藉此機會請他簽名。

▶ I would like to take this opportunity to give a short speech.

我想藉此機會發表一段短短的演講。

抄來抄去都抄這些！
補充例句

Unit 1

Unit 2

Unit 3

Unit 4

Unit 5

Unit 6

Unit 7

以下還有一些「搬遷通知」常用的例句供參考，也可以活用在你的英文e-mail中喔！別忘了，時間、人名等等的地方要換成符合自己狀況的單字或句子。

❶ We will be moving soon.
　我們很快將要搬遷了。

❷ Our new address is as follows.
　我們的新地址如下。

❸ Our fax number remains unchanged.
　我們的傳真號碼維持不變。

❹ We will list directions to our new headquarters in a separate E-mail.
　我們將在另一封電子郵件中列出到我們新總部的交通方式。

❺ We hope to provide you even better services at our new location.
　我們希望能夠在新地點提供您更好的服務。

❻ You could still call me at the same number.
　您還是可以用這個號碼打給我。

4-2 電話號碼變更通知

From lincoln@mail.com
To kidman@mail.com
Subject Phone Number Change

Dear Mr. Kidman,

I am writing to inform [1] you that my office phone number has changed from 02-2666-3412 to 02-2555-7623. You could also fax [2] me with this new number.

Please contact [3] me with my new number from now on, as the old one will be deactivated [4].

I look forward to talking to you as soon as possible.

Yours Faithfully,
Lincoln Burrows

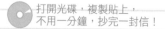

打開光碟，複製貼上，
不用一分鐘，抄完一封信！

★套色的部分為關鍵單字，在右頁可以看到解釋喔！
★劃底線的部分都有相關的文法補充，請翻到下一頁就可以看到囉！

中文翻譯

Unit
1

Unit
2

Unit
3

Unit
4

Unit
5

Unit
6

Unit
7

親愛的基曼先生：

我寫信來是要通知您，我的辦公室電話號碼已從02-2666-3412換成了02-2555-7623。您也可以用這個新號碼傳真給我。

從此以後請用這個新號碼聯絡我，因為舊號碼要停用了。

我期待盡快與您聯絡。

誠摯地，
林肯・波羅斯

抄來抄去都抄這些！關鍵單字　　　　　　⊗□⊖

❶ inform [ɪn`fɔrm] v. 通知

❷ fax [fæks] v. 傳真

❸ contact [`kɑntækt] v. 聯絡

❹ deactivate [di`æktə‚vet] v. 撤銷，關閉

文法重點解析

解析重點 **1**

from now on

from now on是一個很常見、很實用的片語，表示「從現在起」。在非商業的場合也可以用喔！舉例來説：

▶ I promise to be more careful from now on.
   我答應從現在起更小心。

▶ You should treat your husband better from now on.
   你從現在起得對你的丈夫更好才行。

解析重點 **2**

deactivate

activate和deactivate都是在現代網路生活中越來越常用到的單字。在網路上開設帳號的這個動作就叫做activate，而關閉帳號就是deactivate啦！現在需要開設帳號的狀況越來越多，所以大家可要把這兩個單字記好了。在這封信中，deactivate表示的就是舊的電話號碼要「關閉」、「停用」的意思。

抄來抄去都抄這些！
補充例句

Unit
1

Unit
2

Unit
3

Unit
4

Unit
5

Unit
6

Unit
7

以下還有一些「電話號碼變更通知」常用的例句供參考，也可以活用在你的英文e-mail中喔！別忘了，時間、人名等等的地方要換成符合自己狀況的單字或句子。

❶ I've switched to a new telephone number.
我換新電話號碼了。

❷ My new cell phone number is as follows.
我的新手機號碼如下。

❸ You may call this new number starting from next Monday.
從下禮拜一開始就可以打這支新的號碼了。

❹ I will be using a different extension number from now on.
我從現在起將會使用另一支分機號碼。

❺ The old number no longer works.
以前的號碼已經無效了。

❻ My address will remain the same.
我的地址依舊一樣。

4-3 職位變更通知

From smith@mail.com
To cole@mail.com
Subject Replacement Notice

Dear Mr. Cole,

I would like to introduce you to Ms. Sarah Brown. She is replacing me as the superintendent [1] for the Sales Department as of April 10th.

I am extremely [2] grateful [3] for all the support you've given me during my tenure [4]. I hope that you will extend [5] to Ms. Brown the same kindness and assistance [6] you have shown me in the past years.

Yours Faithfully,
Mark Smith

打開光碟,複製貼上,
不用一分鐘,抄完一封信!

★套色的部分為關鍵單字,在右頁可以看到解釋喔!
★劃底線的部分都有相關的文法補充,請翻到下一頁就可以看到囉!

中文翻譯

Unit 1
Unit 2
Unit 3
Unit 4
Unit 5
Unit 6
Unit 7

親愛的柯爾先生：

我想要介紹莎拉・布朗小姐給您認識。從四月十日開始,她將要取代我成為業務部門的主管。

我非常感激您在我任期內給予我的支持。希望您以後也能像過去支持我一樣給予布朗小姐同樣的照顧與協助。

誠摯地,
馬克・史密斯

抄來抄去都抄這些！關鍵單字　　　　　　　　⊗ □ ⊖

1. superintendent [ˌsupərɪnˋtɛndənt] n.
   主管,負責人
2. extremely [ɪkˋstrimlɪ] adv. 非常地
3. grateful [ˋgretfəl] adj. 感激的
4. tenure [ˋtɛnjʊr] n. 任期
5. extend [ɪkˋstɛnd] v. 延伸,給予
6. assistance [əˋsɪstəns] n. 幫助,協助

文法重點解析

解析重點1

She is replacing me

She is replacing me的意思是「她將接替我的職位」，類似的用法還有「She is succeeding me」（她會接替我的位子）、「She is substituting for me」（她會暫時代替我）、「She is filling in for me」（她會暫時代替我）。要注意的是，後面兩者指的都是「暫時」的代替，例如若因請產假、住院等等的理由有一段時間不能擔任該職位時，找一個暫時的代理人，這個代理人做的事就是「substituting for me」、「filling in for me」。

解析重點2

I hope that you will extend to Ms. Brown the same kindness and assistance you have shown me in the past years.

這句不但是叮嚀對方要對Ms. Brown好一點，同時也是藉由「the same kindness and assistance you have shown me in the past years」順便表示對方多年來的照顧與幫助自己都銘記在心，並表達感謝。因此，信中最後收尾處就不必再謝一次對方的照顧與幫助，因為前面等於已經拐彎抹角地謝過了。

抄來抄去都抄這些！
補充例句

Unit
1

Unit
2

Unit
3

Unit
4

Unit
5

Unit
6

Unit
7

以下還有一些「職位變更通知」常用的例句供參考，也可以活用在你的英文e-mail中喔！別忘了，時間、人名等等的地方要換成符合自己狀況的單字或句子。

❶ He will be taking over my current position.
他將要接替我現在的職位。

❷ She will be substituting for me when I'm away.
她將會在我不在時代理我的職務。

❸ I'll be filling in for her while she's in the hospital.
她在醫院的時候我會代理她的職務。

❹ Mrs. Jones will be my replacement.
瓊斯女士將會取代我。

❺ When I'm on maternity leave, please forward all your questions to Mrs. Jones.
我請產假的時候，請把您所有的問題都轉給瓊斯女士。

❻ Mrs. Jones will be my temporary replacement for the next two months.
瓊斯女士會是我接下來兩個月的暫時代理人。

4-4 暫停營業通知

❌ ◻ ⚊

From ted@mail.com
To wills@mail.com
Subject Temporary Closure Notice

Dear Mr. Wills,

I am writing to inform you that our store will be closed temporarily [1] from August 8th to 15th, due to renovations [2] to the interior [3] of the building.

We are planning to reopen on August 16th, and we will be sure to inform you if there are any changes then.

We are deeply sorry if it may cause you any inconveniences [4].

Best Wishes,
Ted Young

打開光碟，複製貼上，
不用一分鐘，抄完一封信！

★套色的部分為關鍵單字，在右頁可以看到解釋喔！
★劃底線的部分都有相關的文法補充，請翻到下一頁就可以看到囉！

中文翻譯

Unit
1

Unit
2

Unit
3

Unit
4

Unit
5

Unit
6

Unit
7

親愛的威爾斯先生：
我寫信是要告訴您，由於我們店內即將重新
裝潢，因此我們將於8月8日至8月15日暫停
營業。

我們打算在8月16日重新開業。如果到時候
有任何變動，我們一定會通知您。

對於此次暫停營業可能給您造成的不便，我
們深表歉意。

誠摯地，
泰德·楊

抄來抄去都抄這些！關鍵單字　　　　　　⊗◻️⊖

❶ temporarily [`tɛmpə,rɛrəlɪ] **adv.** 暫時地
❷ renovation [rɛnə`veʃən] **n.** 整修
❸ interior [ɪn`tɪrɪɚ] **n.** 內部
❹ inconvenience [,ɪnkən`vinjəns] **n.** 不便

文法重點解析

reopen

大家都知道，open是「開」的意思，而前面加一個字首「re-」呢？原來字首「re-」有「重新」、「再度」的意思，因此reopen就是「重新開業」、「再度開張」的意思了。還有一些其他「re-」開頭的單字，例如replay（重播）、restart（重新開始、重開機）、reset（重設）、redo（重做），是不是都含有「重新」的意思呢？

deeply

deep是「深的」的意思，例如要講游泳池很深，就可以用這個字。但變成副詞deeply（深深地）時，通常比較少用來描述物理上的深淺，而是拿來講心理上的「感受很深」，例如此處說deeply sorry，就表示「深深地感到抱歉」。其他的例子還有：care deeply about...（非常深切地關心某人或事）、deeply touched（深深地感動）、deeply moved（深深地感動）等等。

抄來抄去都抄這些！
補充例句

Unit 1

Unit 2

Unit 3

Unit 4

Unit 5

Unit 6

Unit 7

以下還有一些「暫停營業通知」常用的例句供參考，也可以活用在你的英文e-mail中喔！別忘了，時間、人名等等的地方要換成符合自己狀況的單字或句子。

❶ Our shop will be closed from May 1st to the 8th.

本店將在5月1日至5月8日暫停營業。

❷ We will be reopening on January the 1st.

我們會在1月1日重新開業。

❸ We are closing temporarily because the road in front of the store is under repair.

我們要暫時停業，因為店門口的馬路在修理中。

❹ The boutique will be closed for one week as I will be abroad.

由於我將要出國，這家精品店將會暫停營業一週。

❺ We look forward to seeing you at the grand reopening.

期待能在盛大的重新開業時見到您。

❻ When we are under renovation, you may visit our other branch on Market Road.

我們整修的時候，您可以去我們在市場街的另一家分店。

167

4-5 營業時間變更通知

From bc@mail.com
To clients@mail.com
Subject Notice of Change in Business Hours

Dear Clients,

We are pleased to make an announcement hereby [1].

Effective [2] November 3rd, Monday, our new operating [3] hours will be from 9:00 a.m. to 9:00 p.m., Monday to Friday.

We sincerely hope that this change of office hours will allow us to provide [4] the fullest and most considerate [5] service for you.

Yours Faithfully,
BC Book Company

打開光碟,複製貼上,
不用一分鐘,抄完一封信!

★套色的部分為關鍵單字,在右頁可以看到解釋喔!
★劃底線的部分都有相關的文法補充,請翻到下一頁就可以看到囉!

中文翻譯

親愛的客戶：
我們在此有件高興的事要宣布。

自11月3日起，本公司的營業時間將變更為每週一到週五的上午9點至晚上9點。

我們誠摯地希望此次營業時間的變更能讓我們可以帶給各位最全面而周到的服務。

誠摯地，
BC圖書公司

Unit 1
Unit 2
Unit 3
Unit 4
Unit 5
Unit 6
Unit 7

抄來抄去都抄這些！關鍵單字　　　　　　　⊗ □ ⊖

❶ hereby [ˌhɪrˋbaɪ] adv. 在此，特此

❷ effective [ɪˋfɛktɪv] adj. 有效的

❸ operate [ˋɑpəˌret] v. 操作，運作

❹ provide [prəˋvaɪd] v. 提供

❺ considerate [kənˋsɪdərɪt] adj.
　貼心的，周到的

文法重點解析

解析重點 1

effective

effective的意思是「有影響的」、「有效的」。在這封信中表達的是「從……開始生效」的意思,這個用法在告示、通知等正式文件中經常會見到喔!來看幾個例子:

▶ Effective June 1ˢᵗ, all membership holders will receive a discount on all displayed items.

從六月一日起有效,所有會員購買展售貨品都可以打折。

▶ Effective July 16ᵗʰ, those under 12 years old will no longer be allowed to enter this pool without an adult.

從7月16日有效,12歲以下者若無成人陪同不可進入此泳池。

解析重點 2

We sincerely hope that this change of office hours will allow us to provide the fullest and most considerate service for you.

更改營業時間,當然多少都是因為公司自己的考量。然而,大家不可能在給客戶的信中寫一些「因為我們公司人手不足所以要更改營業時間」、「因為大家不想上班上那麼久所以要更改營業時間」之類如此誠實的句子。那該怎麼寫才對呢?像是這一句收尾就是個不錯的作法,讓客戶得到一種「是為了提供客戶們更好的服務所以才更改營業時間的」的錯覺。

抄來抄去都抄這些！
補充例句

Unit 1
Unit 2
Unit 3
Unit 4
Unit 5
Unit 6
Unit 7

以下還有一些「營業時間變更通知」常用的例句供參考，也可以活用在你的英文e-mail中喔！別忘了，時間、人名等等的地方要換成符合自己狀況的單字或句子。

❶ We are writing to inform you about the change of our office hours.

此次來信是要通知您我們營業時間的變更。

❷ Our new operating hours are effective April 4ᵗʰ.

我們新的營業時間自4月4日起生效。

❸ Our new business hours will be from 9:30 to 20:30.

我們的營業時間是早上九點半到晚上八點半。

❹ Our operating hours will be different during the next week.

下週我們的營業時間將有更改。

❺ We will be moving our closing time to 8:00 p.m.

我們的閉店時間將改成晚上八點。

❻ Please note that our new business hours will be in effect starting next week.

請注意我們新的營業時間將從下週開始有效。

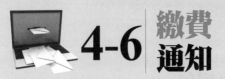

⊗▣⊖

From water@mail.com
To resident@mail.com
Subject Bill Notice

Dear Resident,

This is to notify [1] that you <u>are due to</u> pay a total of \$74 water rate [2] in July.

You may pay through bank transfer [3] (recommended [4]) or bring the enclosed statement [5] to a convenience store and pay the amount [6] there. Please make sure to pay before the 31st of this month <u>at the latest</u>. Late payment [7] will result in cancellation [8] of your water usage [9] until the required [10] amount is paid.

Sincerely Yours,
Water Corporation

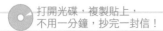

打開光碟，複製貼上，
不用一分鐘，抄完一封信！

★套色的部分為關鍵單字，在右頁可以看到解釋喔！
★劃底線的部分都有相關的文法補充，請翻到下一頁就可以看到囉！

中文翻譯

親愛的住戶：
這是要通知您，您七月必須繳交74元的水費。

您可以透過銀行轉帳（建議使用此方式）或者帶著附上的單子到便利商店付費。請最晚在本月31日之前完成付款。如果遲交款項，您的用水將會被取消，直到所需款項付清為止。

誠摯地，
自來水公司

Unit 1
Unit 2
Unit 3
Unit 4
Unit 5
Unit 6
Unit 7

抄來抄去都抄這些！關鍵單字 ╳ ▢ ▁

1 notify [`notə,faɪ] v. 通知
2 rate [ret] n. 費用
3 transfer [træns`fɚ] v. 轉移，轉交
4 recommend [,rɛkə`mɛnd] v. 推薦
5 statement [`stetmənt] n. 報告單
6 amount [ə`maʊnt] n. 數量
7 payment [`pemənt] n. 付款
8 cancellation [,kænsḷ`eʃən] n. 取消
9 usage [`jusɪdʒ] n. 使用
10 require [rɪ`kwaɪr] v. 要求，需求

文法重點解析

be due to

be due to這個片語的意思是「將要（發生某事）、該要（做某事）」，用在這封信中就是通知人家「該繳錢了」。來看幾個例子：

▶ The coupon is due to expire soon.

這張折價券就快要過期了。

▶ The plane is due to arrive at eight o'clock.

飛機將會在八點到達。

at the latest

片語「at the latest」是「最晚」的意思，用在這封信中就是表達「『最晚』在該月31號『之前』一定要繳交水費」。我們再來看幾個例子：

▶ Please turn in this form before Saturday at the latest.

請最晚在禮拜六之前把這份表格交回。

▶ We'll let you know next Wednesday at the latest.

我們最晚下個禮拜三會通知你。

抄來抄去都抄這些！
補充例句

Unit
1

Unit
2

Unit
3

Unit
4

Unit
5

Unit
6

Unit
7

以下還有一些「繳費通知」常用的例句供參考，也可以活用在你的英文e-mail中喔！別忘了，時間、人名等等的地方要換成符合自己狀況的單字或句子。

❶ This is to notify you to pay your utility bill.
這是要通知您繳納費用。

❷ You can pay the fee through your Internet bank account.
您可以透過網路銀行帳戶繳交款項。

❸ We recommend that you pay through bank transfer.
我們建議您透過銀行轉帳付款。

❹ Please make sure to pay before May 25th.
請在5月25日之前付款。

❺ Please see the enclosed statement for details.
細節請參閱附上的單子。

❻ We will need to receive your payment before May 25th.
我們必須在5月25日之前收到您的付款。

175

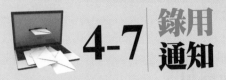

4-7 錄用通知

From novelty@mail.com
To chen@mail.com
Subject Hiring Notice

Dear Miss Chen,

In view of your interview [1] on November 23rd, it is a great pleasure to inform you that you have been approved [2] by the Board [3] of Directors, and the Personnel [4] Department has decided to appoint [5] you as the secretary [6] to our CEO, commencing [7] from December 1st.

We will send you a Notification [8] of an Offer later on. In addition, we will arrange a time to sign the employment [9] contract [10] with you. If you have any questions, please do not hesitate to contact me.

Sincerely Yours,
Novelty Co. Ltd.

> 打開光碟,複製貼上,
> 不用一分鐘,抄完一封信!

★套色的部分為關鍵單字,在右頁可以看到解釋喔!
★劃底線的部分都有相關的文法補充,請翻到下一頁就可以看到囉!

中文翻譯

Unit 1

Unit 2

Unit 3

Unit 4

Unit 5

Unit 6

Unit 7

親愛的陳小姐：

鑑於您在11月23日的面試結果，我非常高興地通知您，您已經通過了董事會的批准，人事部已經決定自12月1日起，聘用您為總經理秘書。

稍後我們會寄給您錄用通知書。另外我們還會安排時間與您簽訂雇用合約。如果您還有任何問題，請與我聯繫。

誠摯地，
新意有限公司

抄來抄去都抄這些！關鍵單字　　　⊗ ▢ ⊖

❶ interview [ˈɪntəˌvju] n. 面試
❷ approve [əˈpruv] v. 批准
❸ board [bord] n. 董事會
❹ personnel [ˌpɝsnˈɛl] n. 人事
❺ appoint [əˈpɔɪnt] v. 指派
❻ secretary [ˈsɛkrəˌtɛrɪ] n. 秘書
❼ commence [kəˈmɛns] v. 開始
❽ notification [ˌnotəfəˈkeʃən] n. 通知
❾ employment [ɪmˈplɔɪmənt] n. 雇用
❿ contract [kənˈtrækt] n. 合約

177

文法重點解析

 later on

later on這個片語的意思是「之後、過一段時間」，用在這封信中就是通知人家「（不是現在，而是）過一段時間會把錄用通知書寄給您」。來看幾個例子：

▶ He said he would come over to visit later on.
他說他待會會過來拜訪。

▶ Let's have dinner first and discuss business later on.
我們先吃個晚餐，之後再來討論公事。

解析重點2
do not hesitate to

句型「do not hesitate to」是「不用猶豫，盡量……」的意思，用在這封信中就是表達「只要有問題都不用猶豫，可以盡量問我」。我們再來看幾個例子：

▶ Please do not hesitate to call me if you run into any problems.
如果你遇到問題，都不用猶豫，儘管打給我。

▶ Do not hesitate to tell me if he's impolite to you.
如果他對你不禮貌，別猶豫，儘管告訴我。

抄來抄去都抄這些！
補充例句

Unit 1

Unit 2

Unit 3

Unit 4

Unit 5

Unit 6

Unit 7

以下還有一些「錄用通知」常用的例句供參考，也可以活用在你的英文e-mail中喔！別忘了，時間、人名等等的地方要換成符合自己狀況的單字或句子。

① I am pleased to inform you that you are recruited.
非常高興通知您被錄用了。

② It's my pleasure to tell you that you have passed the interview.
非常榮幸通知您通過面試了。

③ The Personnel Department has decided to appoint you as sales assistant.
人事部門已經決定任用您為業務助理。

④ We are ready to sign the contract with you.
我們已準備好與您簽合約。

⑤ Welcome aboard!
歡迎加入我們！

⑥ We are looking forward to working with you.
我們很期待與您一起工作。

4-8 假日通知

From admin@mail.com
To staff@mail.com
Subject Holiday Notice

Dear All,

I am very pleased to announce [1] some good news.

To express our appreciation [2] for your hard work this year and give everyone ample time to spend with friends and family, we have decided to close the office from December 25th to January 2nd, <u>inclusive</u>. All personnel [3] will be given <u>paid leave</u> during this period [4].

Wishing all of you a happy holiday season!

Sincerely Yours,
Administrative Department

打開光碟，複製貼上，
不用一分鐘，抄完一封信！

★套色的部分為關鍵單字，在右頁可以看到解釋喔！
★劃底線的部分都有相關的文法補充，請翻到下一頁就可以看到囉！

中文翻譯

Unit 1

Unit 2

Unit 3

Unit 4

Unit 5

Unit 6

Unit 7

親愛的同仁們：
我在此非常開心地宣布一個好消息！

為了對各位一年來的辛勤工作表示感謝，同時也為了能讓各位有充足的時間和家人與朋友一起盡情享受假期，我們已經決定從12月25日至隔年1月2日放假（包括首尾兩日）。這段時間裡，所有員工都將享受帶薪休假。

祝福大家都有個愉快的假期！

誠摯地，
行政部門

抄來抄去都抄這些！關鍵單字　　⊗ ◻ ─

❶ announce [ə`naʊns] **v.** 宣布
❷ appreciation [ə,priʃɪ`eʃən] **n.** 感激，欣賞
❸ personnel [,pɜ·sn̩`ɛl] **n.** 人事，人員
❹ period [`pɪrɪəd] **n.** 期間

文法重點解析

inclusive

形容詞inclusive意思是「包含的」、「在內的」，表達此意思的片語還包括inclusive of。來看幾個例子：

▶ A calendar year is from January 1 to December 31, inclusive.

日曆的一年由1月1日至12月31日，計入首尾兩日。

▶ The monthly rent is $200, inclusive of all utility fees.

月租總共200元，包括一切費用在內。

paid leave

paid leave意思是「照付工資的假期」、「帶薪假」，或者paid holiday。表達各種假期的字詞還包括maternity leave with full pay / paid maternity leave（帶薪產假）、private affair leave（事假）、unpaid leave（無薪假）、sick leave（病假）、maternity leave（產假）、paternity leave（陪產假）等。

抄來抄去都抄這些！
補充例句

Unit 1
Unit 2
Unit 3
Unit 4
Unit 5
Unit 6
Unit 7

以下還有一些「假日通知」常用的例句供參考，也可以活用在你的英文e-mail中喔！別忘了，時間、人名等等的地方要換成符合自己狀況的單字或句子。

❶ We are happy to announce that all staff will be given two additional vacation days.
我們非常高興地向大家宣布，全體員工均將享受多加的兩天假期。

❷ The total number of vacation days will be determined by each employee's length of service.
休假總天數將按照每位員工的工作年資而定。

❸ The vacation is to express our appreciation for your hard work.
此次休假是為了對各位辛勤的工作表達感激。

❹ All employees will be given paid leave during the vacation.
所有員工都能夠享受帶薪假期。

❺ We wish you all a wonderful holiday season.
祝福大家都有一段美好的假期。

❻ We wish everyone a very happy holiday.
我們祝福大家有個非常開心的假期。

4-9 裁員通知

⊗ ☐ ⊖

From abc@mail.com
To benjamin@mail.com
Subject Layoff Notice

Dear Benjamin,

<u>We had been hoping</u> that during this difficult period of reorganization [1] we could keep all of our employees with the company. Unfortunately, we are unable to do so.

It is with regret [2], therefore, that we have to inform you that we will be unable to utilize [3] your services [4] anymore. We have been pleased with the qualities [5] you have exhibited [6] during your tenure [7] of employment, and will be sorry to lose you.

We wish you a <u>promising</u> future!

Yours Truly,
ABC Co.

打開光碟，複製貼上，
不用一分鐘，抄完一封信！

★套色的部分為關鍵單字，在右頁可以看到解釋喔！
★劃底線的部分都有相關的文法補充，請翻到下一頁就可以看到囉！

中文翻譯

Unit 1

Unit 2

Unit 3

Unit 4

Unit 5

Unit 6

Unit 7

親愛的班哲明：
我們一直希望能夠在此次重組的困難時期保留公司的全體雇員，不幸的是這個願望無法實現。

因此，公司不得不遺憾地通知您，我們無法再繼續雇用您。公司一直很滿意你在受聘期間所展現的素質，並為失去您感到遺憾。

祝福您前程似錦！

誠摯地，
ABC公司

抄來抄去都抄這些！關鍵單字　　　　　　⊗ ◻ ⊖

❶ reorganization [ˌriɔrgənəˈzeʃən] n. 重組
❷ regret [rɪˈgrɛt] n. 後悔
❸ utilize [ˈjutlˌaɪz] v. 使用
❹ service [ˈsɜvɪs] n. 服務
❺ quality [ˈkwɑlətɪ] n. 品質，特質
❻ exhibit [ɪgˈzɪbɪt] v. 展示
❼ tenure [ˈtɛnjʊr] n. 任期

文法重點解析

We had been hoping

這裡用了過去完成進行式「had been hoping」，意思是「過去有一段時間中，我們一直希望……」，言下之意也就是「現在」已經不希望了。為什麼「現在」已經不希望了？因為現在的情勢很明顯，不裁員不行了。在這封信中，藉由這一句話帶出後面的主題，也就是要裁員這件事。

promising

動詞promise是「答應」、「承諾」的意思，而形容詞promising是「有希望的」、「前途光明的」的意思。咦？英文那麼像，為什麼中文聽起來沒什麼關係？其實，如果上天對你「承諾」了你的未來一切都會很順利，那你的未來不就是「光明的」嗎？所以其實兩者之間還是有關連的。promising這個形容詞除了拿來描述未來光明以外，還可以拿來描述人事物非常「有前途」，例如a promising singer（很有潛力的歌手）、a promising opportunity（很有希望的一個機會）。

抄來抄去都抄這些！
補充例句

Unit
1

Unit
2

Unit
3

Unit
4

Unit
5

Unit
6

Unit
7

以下還有一些「裁員通知」常用的例句供參考，也可以活用在你的英文e-mail中喔！別忘了，時間、人名等等的地方要換成符合自己狀況的單字或句子。

❶ We regret to inform you that your employment with the firm shall be terminated.
我們很遺憾地通知您，公司將解除對您的雇用。

❷ I regret having to tell you that your service will have to be terminated.
我很遺憾地告訴您，我們不得不解除您的職務。

❸ We are very sorry to see you leave.
我們真的很不希望看到您離開。

❹ Please arrange for the return of company property in your possession.
請安排歸還您所使用的公司物品。

❺ Again, we truly regret to lose you.
我們再一次表示遺憾失去您。

❻ We are very sorry that it has to come down to this.
事情至此地步，我們非常抱歉。

4-10 商品出貨通知

From hans@mail.com
To hopkins@mail.com
Subject Shipment Notice

Dear Mr. Hopkins,
This is a notification [1] of shipment [2].

We have shipped your order No. 3108 as of March 12th, and have also sent you the relevant shipping documents [3] by fax. You should receive the goods you ordered by March 20th if there is no accident [4].

Please let us know when your order arrives. Of course, if for some reason it doesn't arrive, please let us know as well. Thank you!

Yours Truly,
HANS Co.

打開光碟，複製貼上，
不用一分鐘，抄完一封信！

★套色的部分為關鍵單字，在右頁可以看到解釋喔！
★劃底線的部分都有相關的文法補充，請翻到下一頁就可以看到囉！

中文翻譯

親愛的霍普金斯先生：
此為出貨通知。

您訂單號為3108的貨物已於3月12日出貨。
相關出貨資料也已經傳真給您了。沒有意外
的話，您的貨物在3月20日就能收到了。

貨物到達時，請通知我們。當然，如果不知
道為什麼您的貨物沒有抵達，也請通知我
們。謝謝！

誠摯地，
HANS 公司

Unit 1
Unit 2
Unit 3
Unit 4
Unit 5
Unit 6
Unit 7

抄來抄去都抄這些！關鍵單字　　　×□－

❶ notification [ˌnotəfəˈkeʃən] **n.** 通知
❷ shipment [ˈʃɪpmənt] **n.** 裝運
❸ document [ˈdɑkjəmənt] **n.** 文件
❹ accident [ˈæksədənt] **n.** 意外

文法重點解析

解析重點 1
shipping documents

片語shipping document意思是「出貨文件」。
表達「出貨文件」的相關片語還有：bill of lading
（提貨單）、shipping invoice（裝貨發票）、
shipping order（裝貨單）。請看看以下例句：

▶I brought a duplicate of our shipping
documents.
我帶來了我方出貨文件的副本。

▶Could you please fax me the bill of lading?
可以請您將提貨單傳真給我嗎？

解析重點 2
goods

表達「貨物」除了可以用goods之外，「船貨」
可以用cargo或freight；個人訂購的貨品可以
用merchandise（商品）、product（產品）、
commodity（日用品）、item（物品）。請看以
下例句：

▶The store doesn't carry this item.
這家店沒有賣這種物品。

▶Several of the products are on sale right now.
很多產品現在都在特價中。

抄來抄去都抄這些！
補充例句

Unit 1

Unit 2

Unit 3

Unit 4

Unit 5

Unit 6

Unit 7

以下還有一些「出貨通知」常用的例句供參考，也可以活用在你的英文e-mail中喔！別忘了，時間、人名等等的地方要換成符合自己狀況的單字或句子。

1 We're writing to inform you that we have shipped your order No. 3110 as of May 25th.

我們寫信來是要通知您，我們在5月25日已經寄出了您的3110號訂單貨物。

2 Your order has been shipped.

您訂購的貨物已經出貨了。

3 Expect to receive your order in two weeks maximum.

預期在兩週內您會收到貨物。

4 Your order has been shipped to the address listed below.

您的訂單已經被運送至以下列出的地址。

5 Please pick up your order at the convenience store listed below.

請到以下列出的便利商店收取貨物。

6 Your receipt is enclosed in the E-mail.

您的發票已經附在電子郵件中了。

⊗ ▣ ⊖

From horizon@mail.com
To subscribers@mail.com
Subject Notice: Out of Stock

Dear subscriber,

Due to booming [1] sales, we are sorry to inform you that the book you ordered is currently [2] <u>out of stock</u>.

However, we are already in the process [3] of <u>replenishing [4] our stocks</u> and expect to be ready to ship your order to you within three days' time. We are very sorry about the delay in delivery [5], and will include in your package a voucher [6] that can be used in all Horizon Bookstore branches around the country.

Sincerely Yours,
Horizon Books Co.

打開光碟，複製貼上，
不用一分鐘，抄完一封信！

★套色的部分為關鍵單字，在右頁可以看到解釋喔！
★劃底線的部分都有相關的文法補充，請翻到下一頁就可以看到囉！

中文翻譯

Unit 1

Unit 2

Unit 3

Unit 4

Unit 5

Unit 6

Unit 7

親愛的訂購客戶：
由於銷售量暴增，很抱歉通知您訂購的書已經沒貨了。

然而，我們已經在進貨的過程中，預期三天內就能夠準備好將您訂的貨送出。我們很抱歉延遲送貨，因此您的包裹中將附上一張兌換券，可以在全國各地的地平線書局分店使用。

誠摯地，
地平線圖書公司

抄來抄去都抄這些！關鍵單字　　　　ⓧ◻◻

❶ booming [`bumɪŋ] **adj.** 興旺的，繁榮的
❷ currently [`kɝəntlɪ] **adv.** 目前地
❸ process [`prɑsɛs] **n.** 過程
❹ replenish [rɪ`plɛnɪʃ] **v.** 補充
❺ delivery [dɪ`lɪvərɪ] **n.** 送貨
❻ voucher [`vaʊtʃɚ] **n.** 票券

文法重點解析

解析重點 1
out of stock

片語out of stock意思是「無現貨的」、「無庫存的」，意思相當於sold out「賣完」。相對地，表達「有貨」、「有庫存」則用in stock。請看以下例句：

▶ This item is out of stock.
　這個貨品沒有現貨。

▶ This edition is already sold out.
　這個版本已經賣完了。

▶ Do you have any grey pullovers in stock?
　你們灰色套頭毛衣有現貨嗎？

解析重點 2
replenish stock

片語replenish stock意思是「進貨」，replenish意思為「補充」；stock意為「供應物」、「現貨」。除了stock以外，replenish還可以搭配一些其他可以「補充」的詞使用，例如：

▶ We need to replenish our supply of bananas.
　我們得補充香蕉了。

▶ He replenished the cupboard with food.
　他往櫥櫃裡補充了食物。

抄來抄去都抄這些！
補充例句

Unit 1
Unit 2
Unit 3
Unit 4
Unit 5
Unit 6
Unit 7

以下還有一些「缺貨通知」常用的例句供參考，也可以活用在你的英文e-mail中喔！別忘了，時間、人名等等的地方要換成符合自己狀況的單字或句子。

❶ The blue shirt you ordered is out of stock.
您訂購的藍色襯衫已經沒有貨了。

❷ The product is sold out at the moment.
這個產品目前已經賣完了。

❸ In reply to your recent inquiry, the book you mentioned is out of stock.
您近日詢問的書沒有現貨，謹此奉覆。

❹ We will replenish stock very soon.
我們很快就會進貨了。

❺ We expect to ship your order a week later than the original date.
我們預期比原先的日期晚一週送出您的貨物。

❻ We promise to send you your order as soon as possible.
我們保證，會盡快送出您的訂單。

5-1 詢問商品資訊

From hancock@mail.com
To smith@mail.com
Subject Asking for Product Information

Dear Mr. Smith,

We learned from an advertisement [1] that your company produces [2] electronic [3] products of high quality. As electronic products <u>are in great demand</u> in local [4] shops, we are very interested in ordering from you. <u>Is it possible for you to</u> send us a detailed [5] catalogue [6] or any material [7] about your products in terms of price, specifications [8] and payment methods [9]?

Looking forward to hearing from you!

Yours Faithfully,
John Hancock

打開光碟，複製貼上，
不用一分鐘，抄完一封信！

★套色的部分**為關鍵單字，在右頁可以看到解釋喔！**
★劃底線的部分**都有相關的文法補充，請翻到下一頁就可以看到囉！**

中文翻譯

Unit
1

Unit
2

Unit
3

Unit
4

Unit
5

Unit
6

Unit
7

親愛的史密斯先生：

我們從一個廣告得知，您的公司製造高品質的電子產品。由於電子產品在當地的商店中頗為暢銷，我們非常有興趣與您訂購商品。是否可能請您寄給我們一個詳細的目錄，或是任何有關產品價格、規格和付款方式的資料呢？

期待您的回音！

誠摯地，
約翰·漢考克

抄來抄去都抄這些！關鍵單字　　　　　　　⊗ ▢ ⊖

❶ advertisement [ˌædvə`taɪzmənt] **n.** 廣告
❷ produce [prə`djus] **v.** 製作，生產
❸ electronic [ɪlɛk`trɑnɪk] **adj.** 電子的
❹ local [`lokl] **adj.** 當地的
❺ detailed [`di`teld] **adj.** 詳細的
❻ catalogue [`kætəlɔg] **n.** 目錄
❼ material [mə`tɪrɪəl] **n.** 材料，資料
❽ specification [ˌspɛsəfə`keʃən] **n.** 規格
❾ method [`mɛθəd] **n.** 方法

文法重點解析

be in great demand

be in great demand這個片語的意思是「非常受到歡迎、非常暢銷」。demand有「要求、需求」的意思,而既然「要求」很「great」,也就表示有很多人都要求想要這個東西,因此意思就變成「非常暢銷」啦!來看幾個例句:

▶ This kind of tea is in great demand right now.
  這種茶現在很暢銷。

▶ The salesperson told me that these products are in great demand.
  售貨員跟我說,這些產品現在很暢銷。

解析重點 2

Is it possible for you to...?

這是個禮貌的句型,用來客氣地問對方「您有沒有可能……?」多半是用來請對方幫你做某件事。來看幾個例子:

▶ Is it possible for you to carry this for me?
  您有沒有可能幫我拿這個?

▶ Is it possible for you to open the window for me?
  您有沒有可能幫我開一下窗戶?

▶ Is it possible for you to come over tomorrow?
  您有沒有可能明天過來呢?

抄來抄去都抄這些！
補充例句

Unit
1

Unit
2

Unit
3

Unit
4

Unit
5

Unit
6

Unit
7

以下還有一些「詢問商品資訊」常用的例
句供參考，也可以活用在你的英文e-mail中
喔！別忘了，時間、人名等等的地方要換成
符合自己狀況的單字或句子。

❶ I am writing to request information about
your products.
我寫信是想諮詢貴公司的產品資訊。

❷ Your products are well-received locally.
你們的產品在當地很暢銷。

❸ We would appreciate it if you could send
us your catalogue.
如果您能寄來一份商品目錄，我們將不勝
感激。

❹ We've heard that you produce high-
quality electronic products.
我們聽說您生產高品質的電子產品。

❺ This is a very challenging industry, but
with high potential.
這是一個極具挑戰性和發展前景的產業。

❻ We would like some more info concerning
your products.
我們希望能有更多您的產品的資訊。

⊗▢⊖

From davis@mail.com
To brown@mail.com
Subject the Date of Delivery

Dear Mr. Brown,

<u>We would like to know</u> how long it will take for you to deliver our order of May 20th (Order No. 728) for car components [1]. Would it be possible for you to ship [2] our order before early May?

Also, please check if you've already mailed us the invoice [3] of this order, as we've not received it yet. We don't exactly need it in a hurry; we're just asking to make sure that we haven't missed it.

<u>Looking forward to hearing from you soon.</u>

Yours Faithfully,
Henry Davis

打開光碟，複製貼上，
不用一分鐘，抄完一封信！

★套色的部分為**關鍵單字**，在右頁可以看到解釋喔！
★劃底線的部分**都有相關的文法補充**，請翻到下一頁就可以看到囉！

中文翻譯

Unit 1
Unit 2
Unit 3
Unit 4
Unit 5
Unit 6
Unit 7

親愛的布朗先生：

敝公司於5月20日訂購的（訂單號：728）汽車零件，敬請告知什麼時候能發貨。您能不能於五月初之前到貨呢？

此外，請確認您是否已經將此訂單的發票寄給我們，因為我們還沒有收到。我們其實不是馬上就需要啦，只是問一下以確認是不是你們有寄但我們漏掉了。

期待盡快有您的消息。

誠摯地，
亨利．戴維斯

抄來抄去都抄這些！關鍵單字　　⊗◻⊖

❶ component [kəmˋponənt] n. 元件，零件
❷ ship [ʃɪp] v. 運送，送貨
❸ invoice [ˋɪnvɔɪs] n. 發票

文法重點解析

解析重點**1**

We would like to know...

要詢問別人事情，若一開口就說「You must tell us...」（你必須告訴我們……）之類以「You」開頭的句子，容易讓人覺得咄咄逼人。相對地，若把句子的主角換成We，意思改成We would like to know...（我們想知道……），就顯得客氣一些，也不會讓人立刻感到壓力都在自己頭上。再看看幾個這個句型的例句：

▶ We would like to know if you would like to come to the party.
我們想知道您願不願意來參加派對。

▶ We would like to know the location of the meeting.
我們想知道會議的地點。

解析重點**2**

Looking forward to hearing from you soon.

「look forward」這個片語表示「期待」的意思，且期待的事通常是說話者內心已經確定一定會發生的事。然而，對方不見得會很快給予答覆，為什麼寫信者還是用「look forward」，說得一副好像對方一定會很快給予答覆的樣子呢？這也是個帶點小心機的作法，藉由自己「預設」對方一定很快給予答覆的立場，來讓對方感到不好意思，好像不快點回都不行一樣，而盡快回信。

抄來抄去都抄這些！
補充例句

Unit
1

Unit
2

Unit
3

Unit
4

Unit
5

Unit
6

Unit
7

以下還有一些「詢問交貨日期」常用的例句供參考，也可以活用在你的英文e-mail中喔！別忘了，時間、人名等等的地方要換成符合自己狀況的單字或句子。

❶ We can live with the other terms, but not the delivery date.
　我們可以同意其他條件，但發貨日期不行。

❷ We would like to request for an earlier delivery.
　我們希望請您提早出貨給我們。

❸ When will you deliver the products to us?
　你們什麼時候能把商品出貨給我們呢？

❹ Will it be possible for you to ship the goods before the end of September?
　您可能在九月底前出貨嗎？

❺ We really need the order as early as possible.
　我們真的很需要貨盡早送出。

❻ Would you mind delivering our order sooner?
　您介意提早運送我們訂的貨嗎？

⊗◉⊖

From jones@mail.com
To burns@mail.com
Subject Question about your Inventory

Dear Mr. Burns,

You may remember that we've ordered twenty of your digital [1] camera model [2] DSC-T700 last month. It turned out that they sold out in just two days, and now our customers are demanding [3] more.

Please check your inventory [4] to see if you have twenty more for another delivery [5]. Thanks!

Looking forward to hearing from you soon.

Yours Faithfully,
Jack Jones

打開光碟，複製貼上，
不用一分鐘，抄完一封信！

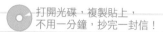

★套色的部分為關鍵單字，在右頁可以看到解釋喔！
★劃底線的部分都有相關的文法補充，請翻到下一頁就可以看到囉！

中文翻譯

親愛的伯恩斯先生：

您可能記得，我們上個月向您訂了20個型號DSC-T700的數位相機。結果它們兩天就賣光了，現在我們的顧客們正急著要更多。

煩請確認該型號是否還有庫存，我們需要再追加20台。謝啦！

殷切期待您的回覆。

誠摯地，
傑克・瓊斯

Unit 1
Unit 2
Unit 3
Unit 4
Unit 5
Unit 6
Unit 7

抄來抄去都抄這些！關鍵單字   ⊗◻⊖

❶ digital [`dɪdʒɪtl] **adj.** 數位的

❷ model [`mɑdl̩] **n.** 型號

❸ demand [dɪ`mænd] **v.** 要求，需求

❹ inventory [`ɪnvən͵torɪ] **n.** 庫存，存貨清單

❺ delivery [dɪ`lɪvərɪ] **n.** 運送

文法重點解析

解析重點1
turn out

turn out這個片語的用法有很多，在此處是當作
「結果是……」、「結果變成……」的意思。我
們來看幾個使用例：

▶ He looked like a good person, but turned out
to be a thief.
他看起來人不錯，結果卻是個小偷。

▶ We ran over to help, but it turned out that we
didn't have to. 我們跑過去要幫忙，但結果其實
不需要我們幫忙。

▶ It turned out that the door was heavier than it
looked.
結果那扇門比看起來還要重。

解析重點2
sell out

sell out這個片語指的是「賣光光」的意思，類似
的片語還有sell like hot cakes（賣得很快、賣得
很好）。我們來看幾個例句：

▶ We went to buy the new game, but it was
already sold out.
我們去買新出的遊戲，但已經賣光了。

▶ I don't understand what's so special about this
book, but it sold like hot cakes.
我不懂這本書有什麼特別的，但卻賣得很快。

抄來抄去都抄這些！
補充例句

Unit 1
Unit 2
Unit 3
Unit 4
Unit 5
Unit 6
Unit 7

以下還有一些「詢問庫存狀況」常用的例句供參考，也可以活用在你的英文e-mail中喔！別忘了，時間、人名等等的地方要換成符合自己狀況的單字或句子。

❶ Would you do an inventory check for us?
能否麻煩您幫我們看一下庫存的狀況？

❷ What type of models do you have in stock?
您的庫存有哪些型號的商品？

❸ Could you check your supply for the commodity we want?
可以檢查庫存看看有沒有我們要的商品嗎？

❹ What products do you have on hand?
您現在有什麼商品？

❺ Could you take inventory and let us know?
可以請您檢查庫存然後通知我們嗎？

❻ Do you mind telling us how much of this product you have left?
您介意告訴我們這個產品你們還剩多少嗎？

⊗▣⊖

From landy@mail.com
To branden@mail.com
Subject Inquiry about Undelivered Goods

Dear Mr. Branden,

We ordered five computers (No. 4879) on February 20th, but we haven't received them yet. Do you mind letting us know when you will be delivering [1] these computers (which should have arrived a week ago)? We desperately [2] need them for our new employees [3].

I'm sorry for rushing you, but if we don't receive the computers soon, we're going to have a huge problem. Please hurry, will you? Thanks a lot in advance.

Yours Faithfully,
Jim Landy

打開光碟,複製貼上,
不用一分鐘,抄完一封信!

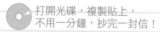

★套色的部分為關鍵單字,在右頁可以看到解釋喔!
★劃底線的部分都有相關的文法補充,請翻到下一頁就可以看到囉!

中文翻譯

親愛的布藍登先生：

我們於2月20日向貴公司訂購了五台電腦（商品編號為4879），但至今尚未收到貨品。您能否告知這些原本一週前就應該到貨的電腦將何時出貨呢？我們急需這些電腦供新員工使用。

很抱歉要催您，但如果我們沒有趕快收到電腦，我們的麻煩就大了。請快點好嗎？先謝謝了。

誠摯地，
吉姆‧蘭迪

Unit 1
Unit 2
Unit 3
Unit 4
Unit 5
Unit 6
Unit 7

抄來抄去都抄這些！關鍵單字　　　✕ ◻ ━

❶ deliver [dɪ`lɪvər] **v.** 運送
❷ desperately [`dɛspərɪtlɪ] **adv.**
　絕望地，拚命地
❸ employee [ˌɛmplɔɪ`i] **n.** 員工

文法重點解析

解析重點 **1**
should have arrived

「should have +過去分詞」是虛擬語氣,這個文法表達的是「過去本來應該做某事(但沒做)」的意思。舉例來説:

▶ You should have told her about it.
你應該要跟她説的。(暗示事實上並沒有跟她説)

用在這封信中此處,即表示「這些電腦本來應該一個禮拜前就要到的(但實際上卻沒有到)」。

解析重點 **2**
desperately

desperately 這個字的中文意思是「絕望地」,但它的「絕望」和我們中文的「絕望」又有一點小小地不一樣。事實上,desperately只是「接近絕望」,還沒有「完全絕望」,還有一點點希望。舉例來説,溺水的人可以很「desperately」地掙扎,因為他還沒有完全絕望(要是真的完全絕望,就乾脆不掙扎沉下去了);而一個對人生完全失去希望準備跳樓的人則不會很「desperately」地跳樓,因為他已經毫無希望了,就不能用desperately來描述。

desperately用在這封信中此處,表示寫信者的公司現在非常緊急地需要這些電腦,要是沒有這些電腦他們會很慘,但他們還不算是完全絕望,畢竟還可以等對方把電腦送來嘛。因此可以使用「desperately」這個字。

抄來抄去都抄這些！
補充例句

Unit
1

Unit
2

Unit
3

Unit
4

Unit
5

Unit
6

Unit
7

以下還有一些「詢問未到貨商品」常用的例句供參考，也可以活用在你的英文e-mail中喔！別忘了，時間、人名等等的地方要換成符合自己狀況的單字或句子。

❶ The products were supposed to arrive three days ago.
商品早在三天前就應該到貨了。

❷ We were informed that we would get the goods within one week.
你們之前告訴我們，會在一個禮拜內拿到貨品。

❸ I was just informed that the product we ordered on September 6th hasn't arrived yet.
我剛才得知，我們9月6日訂的產品尚未到貨。

❹ The products we ordered have not reached us yet.
我們訂的貨還沒有到呢。

❺ If they don't arrive soon, we will be in huge trouble.
如果再不快點來，我們麻煩就大了。

❻ We thought the goods would arrive sooner.
我們還以為貨品會更快到貨呢。

⊗ ▣ ⊖

From topher@mail.com
To william@mail.com
Subject Inquiry about Prices

Dear Mr. William,

I'm writing to ask about the price (freight [1] and handling [2] included) of your newest laser [3] printer [4]. We are very interested in ordering a large number of them, and are therefore <u>hoping for</u> a discount [5]. If we find your product quality satisfying [6], we may continue to make large orders from you in the future.

Your early offer <u>will be highly appreciated</u>.

Yours Faithfully,
Topher Lee

打開光碟，複製貼上，
不用一分鐘，抄完一封信！

★套色的部分為關鍵單字，在右頁可以看到解釋喔！
★劃底線的部分都有相關的文法補充，請翻到下一頁就可以看到囉！

中文翻譯

Unit
1

Unit
2

Unit
3

Unit
4

Unit
5

Unit
6

Unit
7

親愛的威廉先生：

我寫信來是要問您公司最新雷射印表機的價格（包含運費與手續費）。我們極有興趣大量訂購，因此希望能夠打個折。如果我們覺得您的產品品質令人滿意，未來也將會持續向您大量訂貨。

若您盡早報價，我們將相當感激。

誠摯地，
托佛・李

抄來抄去都抄這些！關鍵單字　　　　　× □ －

❶ freight [fret] **n.** 運費
❷ handling [`hændlɪŋ] **n.** 處理，手續費
❸ laser [`lezɚ] **n.** 雷射
❹ printer [`prɪntɚ] **n.** 印表機
❺ discount [`dɪskaʊnt] **n.** 折扣
❻ satisfying [`sætɪsˏfaɪɪŋ] **adj.** 令人滿意的

文法重點解析

解析重點1

hope for

hope for這個片語是「希望……」的意思,後面要
接名詞、動名詞或名詞片語,例如此處的hoping
for a discount就是接名詞片語。再看幾個例子:
▶He's hoping for a promotion soon.
他希望能夠盡快獲得升遷。
▶We're hoping for a sunny day tomorrow.
我們希望明天是大晴天。

解析重點2

will be highly appreciated

這是個被動語態的句型。為什麼要用被動語態,
而不是說「We will highly appreciate...」呢?這
是因為若用主動語態,那麼讓寫信者非常感激的
事物(your early offer)就會出現在句子的最後
面;反過來說,如果用被動語態,Your early offer
則會出現在句子的前面(如這封信中所示)。寫
信者非常希望對方盡早報價,可知「your early
offer」會是這封信的重點,既然是重點,那何不
把它放在句子前面強調呢?因此此處才使用了被
動語態的句型,把重點移到句子的前面。

抄來抄去都抄這些！
補充例句

Unit
1

Unit
2

Unit
3

Unit
4

Unit
5

Unit
6

Unit
7

以下還有一些「詢問價格及費用」常用的例句供參考，也可以活用在你的英文e-mail中喔！別忘了，時間、人名等等的地方要換成符合自己狀況的單字或句子。

① Will you send us a copy of your catalogue, with details of the prices and terms of payment?

請寄給我方一份目錄，並註明價格和付款條件。

② We would like to make an inquiry about this product.

我們想要對該產品進行詢價。

③ We would like to know the price of this product, tax not included.

我們想知道這個產品不含稅的價格。

④ Please send us your quotation for these computers.

請報給我們這些電腦最優惠的價格。

⑤ Please kindly quote us your lowest prices for the furniture.

請報給我們這批家具的最低價格。

⑥ We would like to request information on some prices.

我們想要求一些價格的資訊。

217

⊗ ◻ ⊖

From miller@mail.com
To collins@mail.com
Subject Inquiry about Company Information

Dear Mr. Collins,

I am writing to request [1] some information about your company.

We are planning to invest [2] in your hearing aids because of their excellent performance [3] compared to other similar products. Therefore, we would appreciate any brochures [4] or marketing materials with which you could provide [5] us.

Thank you in advance. I'm looking forward to your reply.

Yours Faithfully,
Will Miller

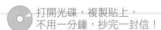

打開光碟，複製貼上，
不用一分鐘，抄完一封信！

★套色的部分為關鍵單字，在右頁可以看到解釋喔！
★劃底線的部分都有相關的文法補充，請翻到下一頁就可以看到囉！

中文翻譯

Unit 1

Unit 2

Unit 3

Unit 4

Unit 5

Unit 6

Unit 7

親愛的柯林斯先生：
我想諮詢有關貴公司的一些資訊。

我們打算投資貴公司的助聽器，因為其性能表現比其他類似的產品都要好。因此，如果您能提供一些簡介手冊或行銷資料給我們，我們將不勝感激。

先謝謝您了，並期待您的來信！

誠摯地，
威爾・米勒

抄來抄去都抄這些！關鍵單字 ✕ ☐ ─

❶ request [rɪ`kwɛst] **v.** 要求，請求
❷ invest [ɪn`vɛst] **v.** 投資
❸ performance [pɚ`fɔrməns] **n.** 表現，性能
❹ brochure [bro`ʃʊr] **n.** 介紹手冊
❺ provide [prə`vaɪd] **v.** 提供

文法重點解析

解析重點 1

compared to

這個片語的意思是「與……比起來」，還有一個很類似的用法是「compared with」。在此處即是用於將收信人公司的產品與別的產品拿出來做比較，用此片語表達「貴公司的產品比其他類似的產品都好」。再看一些使用例：

▶ Compared to John, Jason is very tall.
　跟約翰比起來，傑森非常高。

▶ I know very little about this subject compared to him.
　跟他比起來，我對這個主題瞭解得很少。

解析重點 2

in advance

這個片語的意思是「事前、提前、事先」。用在此信「Thank you in advance」句中，就表示「對方雖然還沒有做出需要感謝的事，但還是『先』謝了」的意思。再看一些使用例：

▶ I wish you could've told me in advance.
　真希望你事先就跟我說了。

▶ We'd have to let him know in advance if we want to use his car.
　如果我們要開他的車，得要事先跟他說才行。

抄來抄去都抄這些！
補充例句

Unit
1

Unit
2

Unit
3

Unit
4

Unit
5

Unit
6

Unit
7

以下還有一些「詢問公司資訊」常用的例句供參考，也可以活用在你的英文e-mail中喔！別忘了，時間、人名等等的地方要換成符合自己狀況的單字或句子。

① I would like to request a copy of your company brochure.

我想要一份貴公司的簡介。

② We are very interested in knowing more about your company.

我們很有興趣想更進一步瞭解貴公司。

③ Is it possible for you to send us some info about your company?

您有沒有可能寄一些您公司的資訊給我們呢？

④ Could you give me a quick introduction of your company?

可以請您很快地介紹一下您的公司嗎？

⑤ Could you provide me some basic information concerning your company?

可以請您提供我一些關於貴公司的基本資料嗎？

⑥ We would like to learn more about you and what you do.

我們想更瞭解你們以及你們所做的事。

221

5-7 詢問 銀行業務

⊗◻⊖

From riley@mail.com
To davidson@mail.com
Subject Inquiry about Bank Business

Dear Mr. Davidson,

Our company is looking for a new bank which will provide us with excellent services at a <u>reasonable</u> [1] cost. If possible, please send us a brochure of your business <u>services</u> and list of fees [2]. After we review [3] the material, we will inform you whether we will open an account [4] in your bank.

I apologize for requesting materials even though we are not yet a client [5] of yours, but we truly [6] hope to become one. Looking forward to your reply!

Yours Faithfully,
Kenny Riley

打開光碟，複製貼上，
不用一分鐘，抄完一封信！

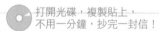

★套色的部分為關鍵單字，在右頁可以看到解釋喔！
★劃底線的部分都有相關的文法補充，請翻到下一頁就可以看到囉！

中文翻譯

Unit
1

Unit
2

Unit
3

Unit
4

Unit
5

Unit
6

Unit
7

親愛的大衛森先生：
我們公司正在尋找一個新銀行，能以合理的
價錢為我們提供優質服務。煩請寄送貴公司
的業務簡介手冊和費用表。等我們確認過資
料後。會通知您是否將在您的銀行開戶。

很抱歉還沒成為你們的客戶就跟你們要資料
了，但我們非常希望能成為你們的客戶！期
待您的回音！

誠摯地，
肯尼・萊利

抄來抄去都抄這些！關鍵單字   ⊗◻⊖

❶ reasonable [`riznəb!] adj. 合理的
❷ fee [fi] n. 費用
❸ review [rɪ`vju] v. 回顧，檢查
❹ account [ə`kaʊnt] n. 帳戶
❺ client [`klaɪənt] n. 客戶
❻ truly [`trulɪ] adv. 非常地，誠心地

文法重點解析

解析重點1

reasonable

想當然，寫信者希望對方報的價格一定是越低越好、越便宜越好，但銀行提供的服務價格大部分浮動性不大，寫信者沒有那麼大的空間可以討價還價，況且在正式信件中直接寫希望對方提供自己「cheap」（便宜的）的服務也顯得太過直接，因此寫信者才選擇了reasonable（合理的）這個字來描述price（價格）。若你收到一封E-mail，對方希望你提供reasonable的價格，你心裡其實大概就要有個底了：對方要的其實不是「合理的」價格，而是「便宜的」價格啦。

解析重點2

services

service這個名詞有時候是不可數的，譬如說若我們要講一家餐廳的服務很棒，就可以說：
▶ The service at the restaurant is great.
　那家餐廳的服務很棒。

然而，若要講「各式各樣不同的服務」，service這個字就變成可數了，後面也可以加s。這封信中，問的是銀行的各種業務，因此用的是可數的service，此處也就可以加s，變成services。

抄來抄去都抄這些！
補充例句

Unit
1

Unit
2

Unit
3

Unit
4

Unit
5

Unit
6

Unit
7

以下還有一些「詢問銀行業務」常用的例
句供參考，也可以活用在你的英文e-mail中
喔！別忘了，時間、人名等等的地方要換成
符合自己狀況的單字或句子。

❶ What services can you offer us?
您能提供我們哪些服務呢？

❷ How much does opening an account
cost?
開一個帳戶要多少錢呢？

❸ What's the procedure of opening an
account?
開立帳戶要辦什麼手續呢？

❹ We will hold a meeting to discuss which
bank is more suitable for us.
我們將會開會討論哪一所銀行比較適合我
們。

❺ We will need more info to decide whether
to open an account with you.
我們需要更多資訊，決定是否要在貴行開
立帳號。

❻ Do you have any brochures on different
account packages?
您有不同帳戶方案的介紹單嗎？

225

5-8 詢問 倉庫租賃

From kendy@mail.com
To carter@mail.com
Subject Inquiry about Renting Storage Space

Dear Mr. Carter,

Our company is interested in renting [1] a big storehouse [2]. It will mainly be used to store a large quantity [3] of products shipped from foreign [4] companies.

Please provide us detailed information concerning [5] the lease [6], including the size and total capacity [7] of different storehouses, and how to go about paying.

Looking forward to your reply!

Yours Faithfully,
Ronan Kendy

打開光碟，複製貼上，
不用一分鐘，抄完一封信！

★套色的部分是關鍵單字，在右頁可以看到解釋喔！
★劃底線的部分都有相關的文法補充，請翻到下一頁就可以看到囉！

中文翻譯

Unit 1
Unit 2
Unit 3
Unit 4
Unit 5
Unit 6
Unit 7

親愛的卡特先生：

我們公司有興趣租用一個大倉庫，主要用來儲存大量從國外公司運進的商品。

請提供我們關於租約的詳細資訊，包括不同倉庫的大小、容積，以及該怎麼付款。

期待您的回覆！

誠摯地，
羅南・坎迪

抄來抄去都抄這些！關鍵單字   ⓧ◻⊖

1. rent [rɛnt] **v.** 租
2. storehouse [`storhaʊs] **n.** 倉庫
3. quantity [`kwɑntətɪ] **n.** 量
4. foreign [`fɔrɪn] **adj.** 國外的
5. concerning [kən`sɝnɪŋ] **prep.** 關於
6. lease [lis] **n.** 租約，租契
7. capacity [kə`pæsətɪ] **n.** 容量，容積

文法重點解析

解析重點 **1**

a large quantity of

quantity和quality是兩個經常一同出現、也很容易搞錯的字。quantity指的是「量」，quality指的是「質」，也就是「品質」。在此處，a large quantity of這個片語就是表示「很大量的」。來看幾個例子：

▶ We have a large quantity of goods waiting to be shipped. 我們有大量的貨品等著要運送。

▶ We received a large quantity of wool from them. 我們從他們那裡收到了大量的羊毛。

解析重點 **2**

go about

「go about V+ing」是「做某事」的意思。那……既然這樣，何不説「doing」就好，幹嘛説一個這麼長的片語呢？原來，go about V+ing含有「著手從事」、「動手處理」一類的意思。舉例來説：

▶ I don't know how to go about asking for their permission.

我不知道該怎麼著手取得他們的同意。

這句的意思就是，説話者連到底怎麼「開始」取得同意都不曉得，他可能在煩惱：我是要寫信去問嗎？寫信的話內容要寫什麼？會不會需要填個什麼單子？他們會同意嗎？我需要付錢他們才會同意嗎？背後有這麼多的煩惱，用doing一個字很難能表達他的「煩惱度」，因此才使用go about這個片語。

抄來抄去都抄這些！
補充例句

Unit
1

Unit
2

Unit
3

Unit
4

Unit
5

Unit
6

Unit
7

以下還有一些「詢問倉庫租賃」常用的例句供參考，也可以活用在你的英文e-mail中喔！別忘了，時間、人名等等的地方要換成符合自己狀況的單字或句子。

❶ We would like to rent some storage space.
我們想要租用儲藏空間。

❷ We would like to learn the specification of your storehouses.
我們想知道您的倉庫的規格。

❸ We would like to know the total area of this storehouse.
我們想知道這個倉庫的總面積。

❹ Please let us know your payment terms.
請讓我們知道您的支付方式。

❺ We would like a spacious storehouse for our goods.
我們想要一個寬敞的倉庫來存放商品。

❻ We would like to know the rental fees.
我們想知道租金費用。

5-9 詢問 訂房狀況

⊗◻⊖

From farrell@mail.com
To affleck@mail.com
Subject **Inquiry about Booking a Room**

Dear Mr. Affleck,

I am writing to book [1] a room for my boss. He will be going on a business trip in your city from March 6th to March 12th, and would like a spacious [2] single room, preferably not on the ground floor, but reachable [3] by an elevator. Please reserve [4] the room under my name. Thank you in advance.

Please let me know if the reservation [5] is successful as soon as possible, for my boss is in a hurry to finalize [6] his travel plans. Thanks! Looking forward to hearing from you soon!

Yours Faithfully,
Daniel Farrell

打開光碟，複製貼上，
不用一分鐘，抄完一封信！

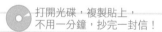

★套色的部分為關鍵單字，在右頁可以看到解釋喔！
★劃底線的部分都有相關的文法補充，請翻到下一頁就可以看到囉！

中文翻譯

Unit
1

Unit
2

Unit
3

Unit
4

Unit
5

Unit
6

Unit
7

親愛的艾佛列克先生：

我來信是要替我老闆預訂一間房間。從3月6
日到3月12日，他將在您的城市出差，想要
一間空間大的單人房，最好不要在一樓，但
電梯可以到。請用我的名字預約房間。先謝
謝您了。

請盡快告知我是否預訂成功，因為我老闆急
著要把出差的計畫做最後的確認。謝啦！殷
切期待您的回覆！

誠摯地，
丹尼爾・法洛

抄來抄去都抄這些！關鍵單字　　　　　　　✕ ▢ ━

❶ book [bʊk] **v.** 預訂
❷ spacious [`speʃəs] **adj.** 寬廣的，空間大的
❸ reachable [`ritʃəbl] **adj.** 能到達的
❹ reserve [rɪ`zɝv] **v.** 預約
❺ reservation [ˌrɛzɚ`veʃən] **n.** 預訂，預約
❻ finalize [`faɪnl̩ˌaɪz] **v.** 完成，最後確定

文法重點解析

single room

飯店有各式各樣的房型，一個人住的話通常是single room（單人房）；而兩個人住的話，可以選擇double room（一張大床）或twin room（兩張小床）。至於三個人的房間則是triple room，四個人的房間是quadruple room。不想記那麼多的話，就直接說a room for three、a room for four就好啦。

ground floor

一般而言，在網路上訂房非常簡單，根本不需要寫一封E-mail給對方，但若你像這封信中的老闆一樣有各種龜毛的要求，就不妨寫封E-mail試試，對方都會很熱心地回答你的。ground是「地面」的意思，那在「地面上」的樓層，當然就是一樓啦！在英國，ground floor就是一樓，而first floor則是ground floor上面的那一層，也就是我們中文所稱的「二樓」啦！接下來就以此類推，second floor是三樓、third floor是四樓……。first floor卻是二樓，這不是很奇妙嗎？所以去英國的話可要注意囉！在美國則不太會說ground floor，first floor就是一樓、second floor就是二樓……以此類推。

抄來抄去都抄這些！
補充例句

Unit 1

Unit 2

Unit 3

Unit 4

Unit 5

Unit 6

Unit 7

以下還有一些「詢問訂房狀況」常用的例句供參考，也可以活用在你的英文e-mail中喔！別忘了，時間、人名等等的地方要換成符合自己狀況的單字或句子。

① I urgently need a room for tomorrow night.
我明晚急需一個房間。

② I'd like a suite with an ocean view.
我想預訂一間有海景的套房。

③ We would like to reserve a double room, please.
如果能幫我們預留一間雙人房，我們將不勝感激。

④ I would like a single room from September 4th to September 10th.
我想要從9月4日到9月10日的單人房。

⑤ How much will breakfast be?
早餐要多少錢呢？

⑥ I would like a room with wi-fi.
我想要一個有無線網路的房間。

5-10 詢問訂位狀況

⊗◻⊖

From lucas@mail.com
To dlairline@mail.com
Subject Inquiry on Seat Reservation

Dear Sirs,

I have reserved a seat on your website [1] this morning under the name Fred Lucas. The flight is from Los Angeles to London, and the flight time is March 16th, 8:00 a.m. My booking confirmation [2] number is E6172. I'm writing to ask whether I would be able to change my seat from a window seat to an aisle [3] one, as I clicked wrong when selecting [4] my seat on the website and can't find a way to change my seat reservation [5].

Sorry about bothering [6] you for something so trivial [7]. Thanks in advance for the help!

Yours Faithfully,
Fred Lucas

打開光碟，複製貼上，
不用一分鐘，抄完一封信！

★套色的部分為關鍵單字，在右頁可以看到解釋喔！
★劃底線的部分都有相關的文法補充，請翻到下一頁就可以看到囉！

中文翻譯

Unit
1

Unit
2

Unit
3

Unit
4

Unit
5

Unit
6

Unit
7

敬啟者：

我在您的網站上用佛雷・盧卡斯的名字訂了
一個位子，是從洛杉磯到倫敦，3月16日早
上8點的班機。我的訂位確認號碼是E6172。
我來信是想問是否能夠把位子從靠窗換成靠
走道的，因為我在網站上選位的時候按錯，
然後又找不到更改訂位的方式。

不好意思為了這麼小的事打擾您。先謝謝您
的幫忙了！

誠摯地，
佛雷・盧卡斯

抄來抄去都抄這些！關鍵單字　　　　　　 ⊗ ▢ ⊖

❶ website [`wɛb,saɪt] n. 網站
❷ confirmation [,kɑnfə`meʃən] n. 確認
❸ aisle [aɪl] n. 走道
❹ select [sə`lɛkt] v. 選擇
❺ reservation [,rɛzə`veʃən] n. 預約
❻ bother [`bɑðə] v. 打擾
❼ trivial [`trɪvɪəl] adj. 極小的，不重要的

文法重點解析

under the name

「under the name」或「under the name of」是表示「用……的名字」、「在……的名義下」。在此處使用這個片語,即是告知對方自己是用什麼名字訂位,這樣對方若真的要幫自己更改訂位資料,有個依據可以比較容易找到他。再看一些這個片語的使用例:

▶ I reserved a room under the name of my boss.
　我用我老闆的名字訂了一個房間。

▶ I signed up under the name "Allie Jones".
　我是用「艾莉‧瓊斯」這個名字報名的。

click

我們在使用滑鼠的時候,「按下」、「點擊」的這個動作就叫做click。過去click這個字的意思是表達「喀答聲」、「喀擦聲」,或當作動詞表達「吻合」的意思,自從滑鼠出現以後這個字的用途就變得更多樣啦。另外,如果要「點擊兩次」,叫做double-click,那「按滑鼠右鍵」呢?可以叫做right-click。這些都是現在電腦時代很常用的詞喔!

抄來抄去都抄這些！
補充例句

Unit
1

Unit
2

Unit
3

Unit
4

Unit
5

Unit
6

Unit
7

以下還有一些「詢問訂位狀況」常用的例句供參考，也可以活用在你的英文e-mail中喔！別忘了，時間、人名等等的地方要換成符合自己狀況的單字或句子。

❶ I would like to reserve a table for two.
我想訂一張兩人桌。

❷ I want to make sure if my reservation went through.
我想確認我的預訂是否成功。

❸ Are there any seats left on the 9 o'clock train to Brighton?
九點去布萊頓的火車還有位子嗎？

❹ I would like to reserve a business class seat.
我想要訂一個商務艙的位子。

❺ I would like a seat towards the front of the bus.
我想要一個靠巴士前面的位子。

❻ I would like to reserve two first-class seats.
我想預訂兩個頭等艙的位子。

⊗ ▣ ⊖

From peters@mail.com
To hostel@mail.com
Subject Inquiry on Specific Rules

Dear Sirs,

I have booked a room in your hostel [1] from next Wednesday (the 12th) to next Friday (the 14th). I'm writing to ask about a couple of hostel rules: are we allowed to smoke on the premises [2]? Can we bring guests into our room (as long as they don't stay overnight [3])? Also, if I return to the hostel after midnight, would that be okay? I thought I'd ask since none of these are specified [4] on your website.

Best,
Paul Peters

打開光碟，複製貼上，
不用一分鐘，抄完一封信！

★套色的部分為關鍵單字，在右頁可以看到解釋喔！
★劃底線的部分都有相關的文法補充，請翻到下一頁就可以看到囉！

中文翻譯

Unit
1

Unit
2

Unit
3

Unit
4

Unit
5

Unit
6

Unit
7

敬啟者：

我在您的青年旅社預訂了下禮拜三（12號）
到下禮拜五（14號）的房間。我寫信來是要
問一些規定：在您的青年旅社可以吸菸嗎？
我們可以帶客人到房間裡來嗎（只要他們不
過夜的話）？還有，如果我超過半夜才回到
青年旅社，這樣可以嗎？我想說還是問一下
好了，因為這些在您的網站上都沒有特別寫
明。

誠摯地，
保羅・彼得斯

抄來抄去都抄這些！關鍵單字　　　　　 × □ —

❶ hostel [`hɑstl] n. 青年旅社

❷ premises [prɪ`maɪzəz] n. 建築物內及周圍

❸ overnight [`ovə·`naɪt] adv. 過夜

❹ specify [`spɛsə‚faɪ] v. 說清楚，標示清楚

文法重點解析

解析重點 **1**

a couple of

大家可能知道,「couple」是「一對」的意思,像是一對情侶、一對夫妻都可以稱作couple。因此,「a couple of」這個片語就有「兩個」的意思,然而後來也漸漸有人把它當作「兩個左右、一些」的意思,也就是說三個、四個也可以稱為a couple of(但一個則不行)。這封信中,寫信中問了三個問題,而他用了a couple of即是要預告自己接下來要問「一些」問題(但不會很多題)的意思。

解析重點 **2**

as long as

as long as 這個片語的意思是「只要……」,可以用在表達「條件」的句型中(例如「『只要』滿足了某條件,『就』……」)。在這封信中即是要表達「是不是只要客人不在這裡過夜,就可以帶進青年旅社來玩呢?」的意思。再來看幾個as long as的使用例:

▶As long as it doesn't rain, we'll have a picnic.
只要不下雨,我們就去野餐。

▶I can edit your essay as long as it's not too long.
只要你的作文不會很長,我就可以幫你校訂一下。

抄來抄去都抄這些！
補充例句

以下還有一些「詢問各項規定」常用的例句供參考，也可以活用在你的英文e-mail中喔！別忘了，時間、人名等等的地方要換成符合自己狀況的單字或句子。

① I have some questions regarding your regulations.

關於您那裡的規定，我有一些疑問。

② I would like to check if I understood some of your rules correctly.

我想確認我是否有看懂您那裡的一些規定。

③ I would like to know the rules before I sign up.

報名之前，我想瞭解一些規定。

④ I would like to ask if bringing these items is allowed.

我想問問看是否允許帶這些物品。

⑤ What are some rules I need to know before applying?

申請前有哪些規定我需要知道的？

⑥ I would like to go over some rules with you.

我想和您一起討論一下規則。

Unit 1
Unit 2
Unit 3
Unit 4
Unit 5
Unit 6
Unit 7

抄來抄去都抄這些！

Unit **6 抱怨篇**

6-1 | 抱怨
商品錯誤

⊗◻⊖

From jackie@mail.com
To bryan@mail.com
Subject Wrong Shipment

Dear Mr. Bryan,

I ordered some products from you (order No. 201314), and received the shipment [1] this afternoon. However, the model [2] of the products I received is not that of what I ordered. I ordered Model SP-520 instead of SP-502. Attached [3] please find the confirmation [4] E-mail (No. 201314) for your reference. I will return this shipment and the freight [5] will be at your cost.

I hope to receive the correct shipment as soon as possible.

Sincerely Yours,
Jackie Black

打開光碟，複製貼上，
不用一分鐘，抄完一封信！

★套色的部分為關鍵單字 在右頁可以看到解釋喔！
★劃底線的部分都有相關的文法補充 請翻到下一頁就可以看到囉！

中文翻譯

親愛的布萊恩先生：

我向您訂了一些產品（訂單號碼第201314號），今天下午收到貨了。然而，我收到的貨物型號和我訂的不同。我訂的是SP-520的型號，不是SP-502。請參考附件的確認信函（第201314號）。我會將這批貨送回，運費由你們支付。

期待能儘速收到正確的貨物。

誠摯地，
潔奇·布萊克

Unit
1

Unit
2

Unit
3

Unit
4

Unit
5

Unit
6

Unit
7

抄來抄去都抄這些！關鍵單字　　　　　　ⓧ◻⊝

❶ shipment [ˈʃɪpmənt] **n.** 裝運

❷ model [ˈmɑdl] **n.** 型號，模型

❸ attach [əˈtætʃ] **v.** 附帶

❹ confirmation [ˌkɑnfəˈmeʃən] **n.** 確認

❺ freight [fret] **n.** 運費

文法重點解析

解析重點1

instead of

「instead of」是個非常常用的句型,它的意思是「而不是……」。出現在它「前面」的東西才是說話者真正想要的,出現在它「後面」的則是說話者不想要的。來看幾個例句就可以明白:

► I wanted tea instead of coffee.

　我要的是茶而不是咖啡。

► You should have been nice to him instead of acting so angry.

　你應該對他好一點的,而不是表現得這麼生氣。

解析重點2

for your reference

這個片語的意思是「供您參考」,your處可以換入其他人的所有格,如their、our、John's等。在常會有許多附件的商業書信中經常會出現這樣的片語喔!看幾個例子:

► Please send us the receipts for our reference.

　請把發票給我們,供我們參考。

► Here are some images for your reference.

　這裡有一些圖片供您參考。

抄來抄去都抄這些！
補充例句

Unit 1

Unit 2

Unit 3

Unit 4

Unit 5

Unit 6

Unit 7

以下還有一些「抱怨商品錯誤」常用的例句供參考，也可以活用在你的英文e-mail中喔！別忘了，時間、人名等等的地方要換成符合自己狀況的單字或句子。

① Please check the purchase order I attached.

請看我附上的訂單。

② Please send us the correct order ASAP.

請盡快把正確的貨寄來。

③ Would you like us to send the products back via freight collect?

您希望我們以對方付運費的方式寄回給您嗎？

④ We're sorry to say that the freight will be at your cost.

很抱歉，運費將由你方支付。

⑤ Attached please find the latest delivery copy.

附上上一次的交貨影本。

⑥ We are looking forward to receiving the correct items soon.

期待能夠盡快收到正確的貨。

6-2 抱怨商品瑕疵

⊗▢⊖

From bill@mail.com
To bobson@mail.com
Subject Defective Merchandise

Dear Mr. Bobson,

We are glad to inform you that the computers we ordered arrived at our company <u>in good condition</u> on June 17th. However, one of the computers we received seems to be defective [1]. The system [2] <u>shuts down</u> automatically [3] a lot for no reason, and sometimes it shows a blue screen [4] when turned on. Attached [5] are some pictures for reference [6].

Your prompt [7] reply will be highly appreciated [8].

Best Regards,
Bill Peterson

打開光碟，複製貼上，
不用一分鐘，抄完一封信！

★套色的部分為關鍵單字 在右頁可以看到解釋喔！
★劃底線的部分都有相關的文法補充 請翻到下一頁就可以看到囉！

中文翻譯

親愛的鮑勃森先生：

我們很開心通知您，我們向您訂購的電腦已經在6月17日狀況良好地到達我們的公司。然而，我們收到的其中一台電腦似乎有點問題。系統常常毫無理由地自動關機，而有時候開機螢幕會變成藍色。附上一些照片供參考。

期待您的快速回覆。

誠摯地，
比爾‧彼得森

Unit 1

Unit 2

Unit 3

Unit 4

Unit 5

Unit 6

Unit 7

抄來抄去都抄這些！關鍵單字　　　　　×□—

1 defective [dɪ`fɛktɪv] adj. 壞掉的，功能不正常的
2 system [`sɪstəm] n. 系統
3 automatically [ˌɔtə`mætɪklɪ] adv. 自動地
4 screen [skrin] n. 螢幕
5 attach [ə`tætʃ] v. 連接，附帶
6 reference [`rɛfərəns] n. 參考
7 prompt [prɑmpt] adj. 立即的
8 appreciate [ə`priʃɪˌet] v. 欣賞，感激

文法重點解析

解析重點 **1**

in good condition

「in... condition」指的是「在（怎樣怎樣）的狀態下」。舉例來說，這封信中的in good condition指的就是「在良好的狀態下」；而in bad condition則是「在不好的狀態下」、in terrible condition是「在很糟糕的狀態下」。看幾個例子：

▶ His health is in terrible condition.
他的健康狀況很糟。

▶ The secondhand car is still in good condition.
這台二手車車況還很好。

解析重點 **2**

shut down

電腦的「關機」、機器的「關機」都可以稱為shut down。相反的「開機」可不是shut up喔！那可就變成「閉嘴」的意思了。如果要把電腦「開機」的話，可以直接說「turn on (the computer)」或「start up」等。那如果要讓電腦暫時休眠呢？可以稱作sleep；重開機則是restart。

抄來抄去都抄這些！

補充例句

Unit 1

Unit 2

Unit 3

Unit 4

Unit 5

Unit 6

Unit 7

以下還有一些「抱怨商品瑕疵」常用的例句供參考，也可以活用在你的英文e-mail中喔！別忘了，時間、人名等等的地方要換成符合自己狀況的單字或句子。

❶ One of the products doesn't work like it should.

其中一個產品並沒有順利運作。

❷ We're having trouble getting your product to work.

我們沒辦法讓這個產品運作。

❸ Can we send the defective product back to you?

我們可以把有瑕疵的產品寄回給您嗎？

❹ Could we send back the defective parts?

我們可以把有瑕疵的零件寄回去嗎？

❺ The shirt I ordered has holes in it.

我訂的襯衫有洞。

❻ There are some light spots on the surface.

產品表面上有淡淡的斑點。

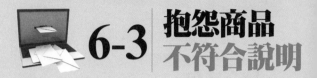

6-3 抱怨商品不符合說明

⊗ ▣ ⊖

From jackson@mail.com
To jones@mail.com
Subject Product Doesn't Fit Description

Dear Mr. Jones,

I ordered your software [1] IT-250 on June 25th, via your online [2] store. However, I'm writing to report that even though it says on the webpage [3] that this software is compatible [4] with Mac computers, I could not get it to even install [5] on my Macbook Air. Suggestions on how to fix this problem will be greatly appreciated.

Looking forward to hearing from you very soon.

Best Regards,
Jane Jackson

打開光碟,複製貼上,
不用一分鐘,抄完一封信!

★套色的部分**為關鍵單字 在右頁可以看到解釋喔!**
★劃底線的部分**都有相關的文法補充 請翻到下一頁就可以看到囉!**

中文翻譯

親愛的瓊斯先生：

我在6月25日透過您的網路商店買了IT-250型號的軟體。然而，我來信是要告知您雖然網頁上寫說這個軟體跟Mac的電腦相容，我卻根本連裝都裝不上我的Macbook Air電腦。如果您能提供建議，教我怎麼解決這個問題，我將感激不盡。

期待您的快速回覆。

誠摯地，
珍妮・傑克森

Unit
1

Unit
2

Unit
3

Unit
4

Unit
5

Unit
6

Unit
7

抄來抄去都抄這些！關鍵單字   ⊗ ▢ ⊖

❶ software [`sɔft,wɛr] **n.** 軟體

❷ online [`ɑn,laɪn] **adj.** 網路上的

❸ webpage [`wɛbpedʒ] **n.** 網頁

❹ compatible [kəm`pætəbl] **adj.** 相符的

❺ install [ɪn`stɔl] **v.** 安裝

文法重點解析

解析重點 **1**

compatible with

片語「compatible with」指的是「與……相容」、「與……相符合」的意思，在現在這個充滿各種新科技產品的年代，懂這個片語就特別重要了，因為科技產品百家爭鳴，在下手購買產品之前當然需要先知道它和自己已有的品牌產品是否相容。我們來看幾個例子：

▶ This flash drive doesn't seem to be compatible with this device.
這個隨身碟似乎和這台裝置不相容。

▶ This app is not compatible with Android phones.
這個應用程式和安卓手機不相容。

解析重點 **2**

get it to

片語「get sth. to」比較口語一些，它的意思是「使……能夠」，後面要接原形動詞。用在這封E-mail此句中，就表示「我連『使它能夠安裝』都沒有辦法」。再來看幾個例子：

▶ I tried and tried but still couldn't get this machine to work.
我試了很多次，還是無法讓這個機器開始運作。

▶ I'm late because I couldn't get my car to start this morning.
我遲到是因為今天早上沒辦法讓車子動起來。

抄來抄去都抄這些！
補充例句

Unit 1

Unit 2

Unit 3

Unit 4

Unit 5

Unit 6

Unit 7

以下還有一些「抱怨商品不符合說明」常用的例句供參考，也可以活用在你的英文e-mail中喔！別忘了，時間、人名等等的地方要換成符合自己狀況的單字或句子。

❶ I just received your product SP-125, but its color is blue instead of green.
我剛收到了您的產品SP-125，但顏色是藍色的，而不是綠色。

❷ This version of software doesn't work on my computer.
這個版本的軟體在我的電腦上沒辦法運作。

❸ The product I received looks completely different from what is shown on the catalogue.
我收到的產品跟目錄上看到的完全不一樣。

❹ The printer I ordered came with the wrong installation software.
我訂購的影印機附上的安裝軟體是錯的。

❺ The dress I ordered is size S, but the one I received is size XL.
我訂的洋裝是S號的，但我收到的卻是XL的。

❻ I'm writing to inform you that the product doesn't work like it says on the site.
我寫信來是要通知您，這個產品和網站上所寫的運作方式不同。

255

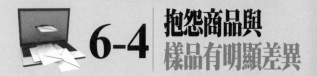

⊗◻⊖

From raymond@mail.com
To james@mail.com
Subject Merchandise Different from Samples

Dear Mr. James,

The product SP-125 we ordered from you last week just arrived at our office. However, I <u>regret to</u> say that they don't look quite like the samples [1] you have shown us. The texture [2] feels very different, and the color is also slightly [3] <u>off</u>. Please re-check this order and send us the right products immediately [4].

Please let me know if you have any questions.

Best Regards,
John Raymond

打開光碟，複製貼上，
不用一分鐘，抄完一封信！

★套色的部分為關鍵單字 在右頁可以看到解釋喔！
★劃底線的部分都有相關的文法補充 請翻到下一頁就可以看到囉！

中文翻譯

親愛的詹姆士先生：

我們上週向您訂購的型號SP-125產品剛剛送達我們的辦公室了。然而，很遺憾地通知您，它們和您展示給我們看的樣品長得不太一樣。材質感覺起來差很多，顏色也有點不太對。請重新檢查這個訂單，並立即寄送給我們正確的產品。

如果您有任何問題，請讓我知道。

誠摯地，
約翰‧雷蒙

Unit
1

Unit
2

Unit
3

Unit
4

Unit
5

Unit
6

Unit
7

抄來抄去都抄這些！關鍵單字　　　　　× □ ─

❶ sample [`sæmpl] **n.** 樣品

❷ texture [`tɛkstʃɚ] **n.** 材質

❸ slightly [`slaɪtlɪ] **adv.** 一點點

❹ immediately [ɪ`midɪtlɪ] **adv.** 立刻

257

文法重點解析

解析重點 **1**

regret to

「regret to」這個片語通常表示「深感遺憾地」、「覺得懊惱地」。在這封信中使用,帶有「我也實在很不想這樣逼你們,可是你們寄來的產品就是不對,我實在沒辦法,所以只好『很遺憾地』告訴您……」的口氣,比較客氣委婉,但同時又能表達不滿的情緒。再看個例子:

▶ We regret to inform you that the conference will be cancelled because of the flu epidemic.
我們很遺憾地通知您,因為感冒大流行,研討會將要取消。

解析重點 **2**

off

大家應該經常看到off這個字,知道它可以表達「下」、「關」之類的意思。不過你可能不知道,它當作形容詞時還有一個用法,就是當作「怪怪的」、「不太對勁」、「不太準」的意思。例如在這封信中,說顏色「slightly off」,就表示顏色「有點不太對」、和樣品看起來不一樣。再看幾個例子:

▶ She seems off today. Is anything wrong?
她今天感覺怪怪的,怎麼了嗎?

▶ This bread tastes a bit off.
這麵包吃起來怪怪的。

抄來抄去都抄這些！
補充例句

Unit
1

Unit
2

Unit
3

Unit
4

Unit
5

Unit
6

Unit
7

以下還有一些「抱怨商品與樣品有明顯差異」常用的例句供參考，也可以活用在你的英文e-mail中喔！別忘了，時間、人名等等的地方要換成符合自己狀況的單字或句子。

❶ Your printer has arrived, but it's a bit bigger than the sample.
您的印表機送來了，但比樣品還大一點。

❷ The sample you've shown us looks to be of better quality.
您給我們看的樣品看起來品質比較好。

❸ The items we received aren't as light as the sample.
我們收到的物品沒有樣品那麼輕。

❹ The ice cream tastes completely different from the sample.
這冰淇淋跟樣品吃起來完全不一樣。

❺ Why does the sample look much more elegant than what we received?
為什麼樣品比我們收到的貨品看起來俐落得多？

❻ The products you sent us are not up to par when compared with your samples.
您送來的貨品和樣品一比，就顯得不夠好。

⊗ ▢ ⊖

From miller@mail.com
To johnson@mail.com
Subject Complaint about Overextended Amount

Dear Mr. Johnson,

I was surprised to receive your bill [1] of the latest orders. According to our agreement [2], your commission [3] should be 5% per order. However, the unit [4] price of our latest orders already include your commission, yet you still added the commission again in the total amount, which means that your commission has become 5.25% in the latest orders.

Please re-calculate [5] and send us another bill ASAP.

Best Regards,
Ryan Miller

打開光碟，複製貼上，
不用一分鐘，抄完一封信！

★套色的部分為關鍵單字 在右頁可以看到解釋喔！
★劃底線的部分都有相關的文法補充 請翻到下一頁就可以看到囉！

中文翻譯

親愛的強森先生：

收到您最新訂單的賬單時，我嚇了一跳。根據我們的協議，您的佣金應該是每份訂單的百分之五。然而，我們最近訂單的價格裡面本來就已經有包含您的佣金了，然而您在總額裡面又把佣金加了一次，結果您在最近訂單的佣金就變成5.25%了。

請重新計算一次，然後盡快寄送另一份賬單給我們。

誠摯地，
萊恩·米勒

Unit
1

Unit
2

Unit
3

Unit
4

Unit
5

Unit
6

Unit
7

抄來抄去都抄這些！關鍵單字　　　　⊗□⊖

❶ bill [bɪl] **n.** 賬單
❷ agreement [ə`grimənt] **n.** 同意，協議
❸ commission [kə`mɪʃən] **n.** 佣金
❹ unit [`junɪt] **n.** 單位，元件
❺ calculate [`kælkjə‚let] **v.** 計算

文法重點解析

解析重點 1

per

「per」是個簡短又好用的單字,意思是「每」,無論生活中或商業上都非常容易看到它。來看看幾個使用例:

one per person 每人一個
two tablets per day 一天兩顆藥
ten dollars per item 一個物品十元
three times per week 一週三次
100$ per hour 一小時100塊
once per year 一年一度

解析重點 2

ASAP

ASAP也就是「as soon as possible」的簡寫,是「盡快」的意思。如果想要表達其他「盡量……」的意思,可以把soon換成其他的形容詞或副詞。例如:

as quickly as possible 越快越好
as cheap as possible 越便宜越好
as early as possible 越早越好
as large as possible 越大越好
as light as possible 越輕越好
as gently as possible 越溫和越好

抄來抄去都抄這些！
補充例句

Unit 1

Unit 2

Unit 3

Unit 4

Unit 5

Unit 6

Unit 7

以下還有一些「抱怨請款金額錯誤」常用的例句供參考，也可以活用在你的英文e-mail中喔！別忘了，時間、人名等等的地方要換成符合自己狀況的單字或句子。

❶ If the bill isn't fixed soon, we'll have to cancel the order.
如果賬單的問題不快點解決，我們就要取消訂單了。

❷ It seems that there's a miscalculation in your bill.
看來您的賬單似乎有誤算。

❸ The date as well as the company name on your bill is incorrect.
您賬單上的日期和公司名稱都不正確。

❹ Please send us a replacement bill as soon as possible.
請盡快寄一張新的賬單給我們。

❺ The amount on your bill seems to be incorrect.
您賬單上的金額似乎不對。

❻ Your total amount on the bill is lacking two zeroes at the end.
您賬單上的總金額最後少了兩個零。

⊗ ▣ ⊖

From collins@mail.com
To thyme@mail.com
Subject Invoice Needed

Dear Mr. Thyme,

We are pleased [1] to inform you that our order PO8110 has arrived in good condition [2]. However, there is no formal [3] Commercial Invoice attached. We already asked the courier [4] agent [5] to look for it through the cartons [6] but nothing was found. Please mail us the invoice immediately. We sincerely hope that this will not happen again as it caused us a lot of trouble in custom clearance.

We look forward to receiving your Commercial Invoice soon.

Best Regards,
Sam Collins

打開光碟，複製貼上，
不用一分鐘，抄完一封信！

★套色的部分為關鍵單字 在右頁可以看到解釋喔！
★劃底線的部分都有相關的文法補充 請翻到下一頁就可以看到囉！

中文翻譯

Unit
1

Unit
2

Unit
3

Unit
4

Unit
5

Unit
6

Unit
7

親愛的泰姆先生：

我們很開心通知您，我們的訂單PO8110已經送達了，貨況良好。然而，沒有附上正式的商業發票。我們已經請運輸代理商把箱子都翻了一遍，但什麼也沒找到。請立刻將發票寄給我們。我們衷心希望這件事不會再發生了，因為這樣造成了我們在海關通關時的莫大困擾。

期待不久後能收到您的商業發票。

誠摯地，
山姆·柯林斯

抄來抄去都抄這些！關鍵單字　　⊗ ◻ ⊖

❶ pleased [plizd] adj. 開心的
❷ condition [kən`dıʃən] n. 狀態
❸ formal [`fɔrml] adj. 正式的
❹ courier [`kʊrɪə] n. 運輸者，信差
❺ agent [`edʒənt] n. 代理商
❻ carton [`kɑrtn] n. 紙盒，紙板箱

文法重點解析

Commercial Invoice

Commercial Invoice在商業英文中翻譯為「商業的發票」，此一單據的用途類似收據，主要是通關用。來看幾個例子：

▶ Our Commercial Invoice is always attached in an envelope that is stuck on the cartons.
我們的商業發票通常附在黏在箱子上的信封裡。

▶ Please send me the Commercial Invoice by E-mail without delay.
請勿拖延，將商業發票用電子郵件寄給我。

custom clearance

custom這個單字原來的意思為「習俗」、「慣例」……等，但此處引申為「通關」。商業貿易上的通關相當重要，如果貨物無法過得了海關，自然也就無法進入國境，不是被退回就是被沒收。請看看下面的句子：

▶ It is necessary to enclose a Commercial Invoice for custom clearance.
貨物通關必須要附上商業發票。

▶ The custom clearance officer asked for a Certificate of Origin.
海關官員要求提供原產地證明。

抄來抄去都抄這些！
補充例句

Unit 1
Unit 2
Unit 3
Unit 4
Unit 5
Unit 6
Unit 7

以下還有一些「抱怨未開發票」常用的例句供參考，也可以活用在你的英文e-mail中喔！別忘了，時間、人名等等的地方要換成符合自己狀況的單字或句子。

❶ Isn't it common sense to enclose a Commercial Invoice for custom clearance?
通關時要提供商業發票，不是基本常識嗎？

❷ It looks like you might've forgotten to attach an invoice.
看來您似乎忘記附上發票了。

❸ Please send us the invoice soon to ensure that you get your payment on time.
請盡快把發票寄給我們，這樣您才能準時收到款項。

❹ We'll need the invoice before we can pay you.
我們需要發票才能付款給您。

❺ We can't find your invoice anywhere, inside or outside the package.
我們把包裹裡外翻遍了，到處都找不到您的發票。

❻ We believe that the invoice you attached might have gone missing on the way.
我們覺得您附上的發票可能丟在路上了。

⊗▢⊖

From martin@mail.com
To lee@mail.com
Subject Complaint about Services

Dear Mr. Lee,

I've been a loyal [1] customer of your supermarket for many years, and what I particularly [2] liked are your excellent product quality and friendly staff. However, I am disappointed to say that one of your staff members (his name tag says "Larry") was extremely [3] impolite [4] towards my mother-in-law yesterday. He called her an old cow because she accidentally [5] stepped on his mop [6].

I don't mean to complain, but do make sure to instruct [7] your employees that such behavior [8] is very bad for the image [9] of any business.

Best Regards,
Tim Martin

打開光碟,複製貼上,
不用一分鐘,抄完一封信!

★套色的部分為關鍵單字 在右頁可以看到解釋喔!
★劃底線的部分都有相關的文法補充 請翻到下一頁就可以看到囉!

中文翻譯

Unit
1

Unit
2

Unit
3

Unit
4

Unit
5

Unit
6

Unit
7

親愛的李先生：

我多年來一直是貴超級市場的忠實顧客，而我特別喜歡貴店優秀的產品品質以及友善的工作人員。然而，令我失望的是，您有個員工（他的名牌上寫「賴瑞」）昨天對我的岳母十分不禮貌。她不小心踩到他的拖把，結果他就罵她是老母牛。

我不是想抱怨，但請一定要告訴您的員工，這樣的行為對任何一家公司的形象都是很不好的。

誠摯地，
提姆・馬丁

抄來抄去都抄這些！關鍵單字　　✕⬜⊖

① loyal [ˈlɔɪəl] **adj.** 忠誠的

② particularly [pəˈtɪkjələlɪ] **adv.** 特別地

③ extremely [ɪkˈstrimlɪ] **adv.** 非常地

④ impolite [ˌɪmpəˈlaɪt] **adj.** 不禮貌的

⑤ accidentally [ˌæksəˈdɛntlɪ] **adv.** 意外地

⑥ mop [mɑp] **n.** 拖把

⑦ instruct [ɪnˈstrʌkt] **v.** 指示

⑧ behavior [bɪˈhevjɚ] **n.** 行為，表現

⑨ image [ˈɪmɪdʒ] **n.** 形象

文法重點解析

解析重點 1

be disappointed to

「be disappointed to...」意思是「很失望地（做某事）」，用在這封信中此處即「帶著失望的心情投訴服務不周」。和disappointed長得很像的一個形容詞是disappointing，兩者的不同在於前者用於形容人的感情「覺得失望」，而後者則是用於形容人事物「令人失望」。可不要搞混了喔！來看看下面的例子比較一下：

▶ I'm disappointed to learn that they lost the game.

得知他們輸了比賽，我很失望。

▶ The movie was boring and disappointing.

這部電影很無聊，令人失望。

解析重點 2

name tag

name tag指的是工作人員或學生、營隊成員等掛在身上的「名牌」。tag的意思就是「標籤」、「吊牌」，像大家在使用社群網站的時候，不是也常需要把親朋好友「標記」在文章或照片中嗎？這時英文就是用「tag」這個字。對了，那麼工作上常用的「名片」呢？通常不會稱為name card（雖然你這樣講大家應該還是懂你的意思），而是稱為business card。

抄來抄去都抄這些！
補充例句

Unit
1

Unit
2

Unit
3

Unit
4

Unit
5

Unit
6

Unit
7

以下還有一些「抱怨服務不周」常用的例句供參考，也可以活用在你的英文e-mail中喔！別忘了，時間、人名等等的地方要換成符合自己狀況的單字或句子。

❶ Your food was good, but the service was horrible.
你們的菜很好吃，但服務非常糟糕。

❷ I'm writing to complain about one of your waiters.
我寫信來是要抱怨你們的一個服務生。

❸ The service quality in your restaurant makes me cringe.
你們餐廳的服務品質真是糟透了。

❹ You really need to hire a more attentive front desk clerk.
你們真的很需要請一個注意力比較集中的前台人員。

❺ One of your operators was very impolite when answering my call.
你們有個接線人員在接我的電話時非常不禮貌。

❻ You'll need to educate your employees better if you don't want to lose more customers.
如果不想失去更多顧客，你們必須教育好你們的員工。

271

⊗◻⊖

From williams@mail.com
To kent@mail.com
Subject Contract Violation

Dear Mr. Kent,

Attached is our contract[1] of purchasing[2] order PO0801 for your reference. Your company has not been sending us the products as detailed[3] in the contract, and this has caused us a lot of inconvenience[4] for several months. I'm afraid that if this continues[5], we will have to resort to legal action.

Please contact me directly[6] if you have any questions.

Best Regards,
Bentley Williams

打開光碟，複製貼上，
不用一分鐘，抄完一封信！

★套色的部分為關鍵單字 在右頁可以看到解釋喔！
★劃底線的部分都有相關的文法補充 請翻到下一頁就可以看到囉！

中文翻譯

Unit
1

Unit
2

Unit
3

Unit
4

Unit
5

Unit
6

Unit
7

親愛的肯特先生：

附件是我們訂購單號PO0801的合約供您參考。您的公司並未像合約中所列地寄送貨品給我們，這造成了我們很大的不便。如果這個情況持續下去，恐怕我們就得尋求法律途徑了。

如果有什麼問題，請直接和我們聯絡。

誠摯地，
班利・威廉斯

抄來抄去都抄這些！關鍵單字　　　　✕ ☐ ⊖

❶ contract [kən`trækt] **n.** 合約
❷ purchase [`pɝtʃəs] **v.** 購買
❸ detail [`ditel] **v.** 詳細條列出
❹ inconvenience [ˌɪnkən`vinjəns] **n.** 不便
❺ continue [kən`tɪnjʊ] **v.** 持續
❻ directly [də`rɛktlɪ] **adv.** 直接地

273

文法重點解析

I'm afraid that

「I'm afraid that...」句型意思是「恐怕……」，常用於書信中，尤其適合用在「你想要告知壞消息但又想要婉轉客氣點」的時候。例如這封信中，寫信者對於對方違約想當然是很不開心的，不開心到已經打算要上法院的程度，但又礙於做人要客氣，他不能直接說「那咱們法院見」，只好利用I'm afraid that...句型來婉轉地說「如果再不改善的話，那恐怕就要尋求法律管道囉」。如果你也遇到這種令你不悅但又必須客氣表達的狀況，不妨也使用這個句型試試看吧！

resort to

「resort to」是個蠻有趣的片語，它的意思是「不得不（使出某種手段）」、「被逼得必須（做某事）」。例如在這封信中，使用這個片語就是要表示「我們『不得不』尋求法律途徑，這可是你逼我們的，我們也是萬分不願意啊」。以下再看幾個例子：

▶ As there's nothing to eat, we have to resort to making cup noodles. 因為沒有東西可以吃，我們只好不得不煮泡麵了。

▶ Having no money, he resorted to stealing from passers-by.
他沒有錢，於是不得不偷路人的錢。

抄來抄去都抄這些！
補充例句

Unit 1

Unit 2

Unit 3

Unit 4

Unit 5

Unit 6

Unit 7

以下還有一些「抱怨違反合約」常用的例句供參考，也可以活用在你的英文e-mail中喔！別忘了，時間、人名等等的地方要換成符合自己狀況的單字或句子。

❶ It is stated in the contract that any delays require financial compensation.
在合約中指出，任何延遲都必須以金錢賠償。

❷ We're sorry to inform you that you've violated Item 02 in the contract.
很抱歉通知您，您違反了合約的第二項目。

❸ If this continues, we regret to say that we have to bring this to court.
如果這個狀況持續，我們必須很抱歉地說，我們將要告上法庭了。

❹ Your violation of the contract is really a huge inconvenience to us.
您的違約對我們來說真的是很大的不便。

❺ Please make sure to follow our agreement detailed in the contract.
請一定要遵守我們在合約中列出的協議。

❻ If this happens again, we will not hesitate to sue.
如果這種事再發生，我們會毫不猶豫地告上法庭。

6-9 抱怨 遲交貨品

From alberts@mail.com
To cole@mail.com
Subject Complaint about Delayed Shipment

Dear Mr. Cole,

Our order (purchasing order PO0908) was scheduled to be sent to us by the end of last December. You postponed [1] this shipment [2] to January 6th because of "insufficient [3] accessories [4]". On January 15th this shipment was again postponed due to "terrible weather". We've had enough of your excuses [5]. Please ship our order at once, and let me know when it will arrive at our factory. Your delaying [6] tactics [7] have caused [8] us enough problems already and we want no more of that.

Best Regards,
David Alberts

打開光碟，複製貼上，
不用一分鐘，抄完一封信！

★套色的部分為關鍵單字 在右頁可以看到解釋喔！
★劃底線的部分都有相關的文法補充 請翻到下一頁就可以看到囉！

中文翻譯

Unit 1

Unit 2

Unit 3

Unit 4

Unit 5

Unit 6

Unit 7

親愛的柯爾先生：

我們訂的貨品（訂購單PO0908）本來預計在去年十二月底就要寄給我們。您將出貨日期改至1月6日，因為「零件不足」。在1月15日，又再延期一次，因為「天氣很差」。我們已經受夠您的藉口了。請立刻將我們的訂單出貨，並讓我知道何時會抵達我們的工廠。您的拖延戰術已經造成我們夠多問題了，我們不希望你們繼續拖延。

誠摯地，

大衛‧亞伯特

抄來抄去都抄這些！關鍵單字 ⊗□⊖

❶ postpone [post`pon] v. 延後，延期

❷ shipment [`ʃɪpmənt] n. 運貨

❸ insufficient [ˌɪnsə`fɪʃənt] adj. 不夠的

❹ accessory [æk`sɛsərɪ] n. 零件，配件

❺ excuse [ɪk`skjuz] n. 藉口

❻ delay [dɪ`le] v. 延後，延期

❼ tactic [`tæktɪk] n. 技巧

❽ cause [kɔz] v. 造成

文法重點解析

"insufficient accessories"

insufficient accessories直翻就是「零件不足」的意思。那麼它為什麼旁邊要加「" "」的標點呢?下面的「terrible weather」為什麼也加上了這樣的標點呢?其實這表示寫信者是在引用對方說過的話,也就是說「insufficient accessories」和「terrible weather」是對方給的藉口,而寫信者受不了了,於是刻意加上引號強調這些字眼,頗有「什麼insufficient accessories、terrible weather,你們自己看看你們找這什麼爛藉口」的味道。若你想要在信中引用對方說過的話,也可以使用引號喔!

had enough of

「have enough of」這個片語是「受夠了」的意思,後面接人、事、物都可以喔!來看幾個例子:

▶ I have had enough of George.
我受夠喬治了。(接「人」)

▶ I have had enough of George's complaining.
我受夠喬治一直抱怨了。(接「事」)

▶ I have had enough of George's alarm clock.
我受夠喬治的鬧鐘了。(接「物」)

抄來抄去都抄這些！
補充例句

Unit 1

Unit 2

Unit 3

Unit 4

Unit 5

Unit 6

Unit 7

以下還有一些「抱怨遲交貨品」常用的例句供參考，也可以活用在你的英文e-mail中喔！別忘了，時間、人名等等的地方要換成符合自己狀況的單字或句子。

❶ Your continuous delays are causing us lots of problems.
您一直拖延造成了我們不少問題。

❷ If you still insist on not shipping our order, we're afraid that we will no longer order from you.
如果您依舊不出貨，我們恐怕就不會再向您訂貨了。

❸ If you keep postponing the delivery, we might have to ask for a refund.
如果您一直延期交貨，我們只好要求退費了。

❹ All this postponing violates what is stated in our contract.
您一直延期，這已經違反了我們合約中的條例。

❺ We're afraid we have to terminate the contract if you don't ship our order on time.
如果您不準時交貨，我們將要撤銷合約了。

❻ I'm writing to let you know that we're quite unhappy with your delaying.
我寫信是要告知您我們對您的延遲非常不開心。

279

6-10 抱怨太晚處理要求

From quinn@mail.com
To mann@mail.com
Subject Complaint about Delayed Request

Dear Mr. Mann,

I would like to inquire [1] if you have sent us the Supermarket Catalogue [2] we requested [3] three weeks ago. We don't seem to have received it yet. Is there a problem? If not, please make sure to send it as soon as possible, or else we might have to consider [4] products from other supermarkets instead.

We really do hope to purchase from you, but we're afraid that it won't be possible if we don't receive the catalogue soon enough. Your prompt [5] response [6] will be appreciated.

Best Regards,
Al Quinn

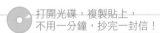

打開光碟，複製貼上，
不用一分鐘，抄完一封信！

★套色的部分為關鍵單字 在右頁可以看到解釋喔！
★劃底線的部分都有相關的文法補充 請翻到下一頁就可以看到囉！

中文翻譯

親愛的曼恩先生：

我想詢問您是否已經將我們三週前請您寄來的超級市場產品目錄送出了。我們似乎還沒收到的樣子。是出了什麼問題嗎？如果沒問題，請盡快送出，否則我們可能就必須考慮其他超級市場的產品了。

我們真的很希望向你們購買產品，但恐怕如果我們無法夠快收到目錄，就沒辦法向你們買了。若您盡快回覆，我們將不勝感激。

誠摯地，
艾爾・昆恩

Unit
1
Unit
2
Unit
3
Unit
4
Unit
5
Unit
6
Unit
7

抄來抄去都抄這些！關鍵單字　　　　　　　　❌ ▢ ━

1 inquire [ɪn`kwaɪr] v. 詢問
2 catalogue [`kætəlɔg] n. 目錄
3 request [rɪ`kwɛst] v. 要求，請求
4 consider [kən`sɪdɚ] v. 考慮
5 prompt [prɑmpt] adj. 立即的
6 response [rɪ`spɑns] n. 回覆，答覆

文法重點解析

解析重點 **1**

Is there a problem?

「Is there a problem?」的意思是「有什麼問題嗎？」、「出了什麼問題嗎？」，它的使用情境很廣，搭配你的表情可以表達很多不同的意思，例如若你搭配關心的表情，它就是一句關切的問候，若你搭配兇狠的表情，就是要找碴的人滾遠點。在這封信中由於從頭到尾並沒有出現太過兇狠的態度，收信人應可以判別是關切的表現，帶點「是否出了什麼問題？如果有問題，我們也理解，不會一直寫信叨擾您」的語氣，是個禮貌中帶點關切的問法。如果你也要在書信中用這一句，別忘了上下文的語氣要委婉客氣喔！

解析重點 **2**

or else

這個句型是「不然……」、「否則……」的意思。在這封信中，即是語氣強烈地用來表示「你們快點送目錄來，不然我們只好找別人囉」的警告意思。在口語中，它的後面有時候會什麼也不接，直接讓對方想像「不然會怎樣」，頗有威脅的意味。例如：

▶ You'd better not touch my girlfriend, or else!
你最好別碰我女朋友，不然結果你自己知道！
（當然這個用法在正式書信中是不能出現的。）

抄來抄去都抄這些！
補充例句

Unit 1

Unit 2

Unit 3

Unit 4

Unit 5

Unit 6

Unit 7

以下還有一些「抱怨太晚處理要求」常用的例句供參考，也可以活用在你的英文e-mail中喔！別忘了，時間、人名等等的地方要換成符合自己狀況的單字或句子。

❶ We understand that you must be busy, but we don't see why this small request is taking forever.

您一定很忙，我們瞭解，但我們不懂為什麼這個小小的要求要花這麼久。

❷ It's been a month and our request still hasn't been processed.

已經一個月了，我們的要求卻還沒處理。

❸ Please let us know when you will send us what we need.

請告知我們您何時會送出我們需要的東西。

❹ Our request form still hasn't been processed yet.

我們的需求單還沒有處理呢。

❺ I'm wondering if you did get my E-mail detailing what we need from you.

不曉得您有沒有收到我們需要您幫忙的事項的電子郵件。

❻ I don't see why the request is taking so long to deal with.

我不懂為什麼這個要求要花那麼久來處理。

6-11 抱怨
訂單錯誤

⊗◉⊖

From hoffman@mail.com
To dalton@mail.com
Subject Complaint about Incorrect Shipment

Dear Mr. Dalton,

As you may know, we ordered ten timer [1] devices [2] (No. PO0970) from you last week. This afternoon, we received a package from you, but opened it to find ten toy cars! Yes, the cars are cute <u>and everything</u>, but they just aren't what we ordered. As we've already mercilessly [3] ripped [4] open the package (naturally, since we have to open a package to learn what's in it) <u>there's no way</u> we can send it back to you the way it was when it came. What should we do about those cars? We'd appreciate your prompt response, unless you want us to keep them for personal [5] enjoyment [6] of course.

Best Regards,
Richard Hoffman

打開光碟，複製貼上，
不用一分鐘，抄完一封信！

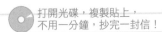

★套色的部分為關鍵單字 在右頁可以看到解釋喔！
★劃底線的部分都有相關的文法補充 請翻到下一頁就可以看到囉！

中文翻譯

Unit
1

Unit
2

Unit
3

Unit
4

Unit
5

Unit
6

Unit
7

親愛的道爾吞先生：

如您所知，我們上週向您訂購了十個計時器（訂單號PO0970）。今天下午我們收到了你們寄來的包裹，打開一看是十台玩具小汽車！是的，這些小汽車是很可愛啦，但我們訂的就不是小汽車啊。因為我們已經狠狠地把包裹撕開了（這也是當然的，因為要打開包裹才能知道裡面有什麼），我們不可能把包裹完好如初地寄回去。那這些車子我們該怎麼辦？若您能盡快回覆，我們將不勝感激。當然如果你們想把小汽車送我們當作個人娛樂之用我們也不介意。

誠摯地，

理查·霍夫曼

抄來抄去都抄這些！關鍵單字　　　　　　⊗ ◻ ⊖

❶ timer [`taɪmə] n. 計時器

❷ device [dɪ`vaɪs] n. 儀器，器具

❸ mercilessly [`mɝsɪlɪslɪ] adv.
　　毫不憐憫地，狠狠地

❹ rip [rɪp] v. 撕

❺ personal [`pɝsn̩l] adj. 個人的，私人的

❻ enjoyment [ɪn`dʒɔɪmənt] n. 享受，娛樂

文法重點解析

解析重點1
and everything

由整封信的口氣可以看出,這位寫信者應該與收信者的關係不錯,因此可以用非常輕鬆的語氣寫信,並順便開對方送錯貨的玩笑。「and everything」是個相當口語的用法,意近「還有很多,我就不一一列舉了」,後面通常接上「但是」一類的轉折,如這封信中即是表示「小汽車很可愛,還有很多其他的好處,你也知道,我就不說了,『但是』我們訂的又不是小汽車」。再看幾個例子:

▶ She's nice and everything, but really not my type. 她是人很好沒錯啦,但實在不是我的菜。

▶ I understand you're busy and everything, but it will take you less than a second. 我知道你是很忙啦那些的,但這只會花你不到一秒喔。

解析重點2
there's no way

這也是個有點口語的句型,意為「絕不可能」、「絕對做不到」。此處寫信者是要利用此句型表達「包裹都撕爛了,又拼不回去,我們絕不可能把包裹恢復原狀送回去給您」。再看幾個例子:

▶ There's no way Pete and John are brothers! 彼得跟約翰絕不可能是兄弟!

▶ I don't even know him. There's no way we can be friends.
我根本不認識他,我們絕不可能是朋友。

抄來抄去都抄這些！
補充例句

以下還有一些「抱怨訂單錯誤」常用的例句供參考，也可以活用在你的英文e-mail中喔！別忘了，時間、人名等等的地方要換成符合自己狀況的單字或句子。

Unit 1

Unit 2

Unit 3

Unit 4

Unit 5

Unit 6

Unit 7

❶ We received a package from you, but a different company name is written on it.
我們收到了您的包裹，但上面寫的是不同的公司名稱。

❷ You sent us something that should have gone to someone else.
你們把本來該寄給別人的東西寄給我們了。

❸ We're sorry to hear that our order is sent to another address by accident.
我們很遺憾聽說我們的訂單不小心被寄到別的地址去了。

❹ We received something we didn't order.
我們收到了明明沒訂的東西。

❺ We're wondering if the wine we received is meant for someone else.
我們想知道我們收到的酒是不是應該是別人的。

❻ If we received someone else's order, where did our order go?
如果我們收到了其他人的訂單，那我們的訂單跑哪去了？

抄來抄去都抄這些！

Unit **7**
恭賀與
慰問篇

7-1 恭賀 新生子女

From clark@mail.com
To brown@mail.com
Subject Congratulations on your Baby Boy!

Dear Mr. Brown,

Please accept our wholehearted [1] congratulations [2] on the safe arrival [3] of your baby boy. We are sure you'll make a wonderful father.

We are glad to hear that the mother and baby are both doing well. We can hardly wait to hug [4] the baby and show the little darling [5] the gifts we've bought him! Have you decided on a name yet? Let us know when you've decided; we'd like to embroider [6] his name on the baby napkin [7] we got for him.

Affectionately Yours,
Tom and Felicity Clark

打開光碟，複製貼上，
不用一分鐘，抄完一封信！

★套色的部分為關鍵單字 在右頁可以看到解釋喔！
★劃底線的部分都有相關的文法補充 請翻到下一頁就可以看到囉！

Unit
1

Unit
2

Unit
3

Unit
4

Unit
5

Unit
6

Unit
7

中文翻譯

親愛的布朗先生：

衷心恭賀您的男嬰平安出生了。我們相信您將會是個很棒的父親。

我們很開心聽說母子均安。我們等不及要抱抱寶寶、讓那個小可愛看看我們買給他的禮物了！你們決定名字了嗎？決定了請告訴我們，我們想要把他的名字繡在要送他的寶寶小毛巾上。

誠摯地，
湯姆＆費利希蒂・克拉克

抄來抄去都抄這些！關鍵單字　　　　　　　⊗◻◺

❶ wholehearted [`hol`hɑrtɪd] **adj.** 全心全意的
❷ congratulation [kən͵grætʃə`leʃən] **n.** 恭喜
❸ arrival [ə`raɪvl] **n.** 抵達
❹ hug [hʌg] **v.** 擁抱
❺ darling [`dɑrlɪŋ] **n.** 親愛的，寵兒
❻ embroider [ɪm`brɔɪdə] **v.** 刺繡
❼ napkin [`næpkɪn] **n.** 紙巾，小毛巾

文法重點解析

do well

「do well」這個片語的意思是指「狀況很好、很順利」，在這封信中指的是媽媽和寶寶的健康方面狀況很好，但也可以拿來指生意狀況很好、生活很愉快、事情做得很順利、表現得很好等等。來看幾個例子：

▶ I thought you did very well during the performance.
我覺得你在演出時表現得很好。

▶ I'm doing well; thanks for asking.
我一切都很好，謝謝你問起。

decide on

「decide on」後面接名詞或名詞片語、名詞子句、或動名詞，意思是「下決定」，例如在這封信中就是用來表達「決定寶寶的名字是什麼」。再來看一些例子：

▶ I can't decide on which dress to wear to the party.
我沒辦法決定要穿哪件洋裝去派對。

▶ They've finally decided on the location for their new building.
他們終於決定了新大樓的地點。

抄來抄去都抄這些！

補充例句

Unit 1

Unit 2

Unit 3

Unit 4

Unit 5

Unit 6

Unit 7

以下還有一些「恭賀新生子女」常用的例句供參考，也可以活用在你的英文e-mail中喔！別忘了，時間、人名等等的地方要換成符合自己狀況的單字或句子。

❶ We're excited to hear about your new baby girl.

聽說您有了個女兒，我們非常興奮。

❷ We're positive that you'll be the best mother ever.

我們相信妳將會是最棒的母親。

❸ We are only too eager to see your new baby.

我們等不及要見見您的新寶寶了。

❹ Congratulations! You're going to be a father!

恭喜你！你要當爸爸了！

❺ All the best to you and your new baby.

祝福您與小寶寶幸福。

❻ Congratulations for giving birth to the most adorable little thing!

恭喜您生了最可愛的孩子！

7-2 | 恭賀升遷

⊗ ▣ ⊖

From ray@mail.com
To greene@mail.com
Subject Congratulations on your Promotion!

Dear Mr. Greene,
I am very delighted [1] to hear that you have been promoted [2] to manager [3] position [4] in the Sales Department. It is an outstanding [5] achievement [6] in a very <u>competitive</u> field, and I would like to offer my warmest congratulations.

My colleagues [7] join me in wishing you happiness and success in the important responsibilities [8] that <u>lie before you</u>.

Sincerely Yours,
Thomas Ray

打開光碟，複製貼上，
不用一分鐘，抄完一封信！

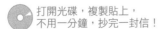

★套色的部分**為關鍵單字** 在右頁可以看到解釋喔！
★劃底線的部分**都有相關的文法補充** 請翻到下一頁就可以看到囉！

中文翻譯

親愛的格林先生：

我很開心聽說您被升格為業務部主管了。在這一個競爭這麼激烈的領域，這是個很傑出的成就，我想給予您最溫暖的祝賀。

我的同事們也和我一樣祝您幸福，並且在你未來將面對到的責任上一切順利。

誠摯地，
湯瑪斯·雷

Unit 1
Unit 2
Unit 3
Unit 4
Unit 5
Unit 6
Unit 7

抄來抄去都抄這些！關鍵單字　　⊗□⊖

1 delighted [dɪ`laɪtɪd] **adj.** 開心的
2 promote [prə`mot] **v.** 晉升
3 manager [`mænɪdʒɚ] **n.** 主管
4 position [pə`zɪʃən] **n.** 位階，位置，職位
5 outstanding [`aʊt`stændɪŋ] **adj.**
　出色的，傑出的
6 achievement [ə`tʃivmənt] **n.** 成就
7 colleague [kɑ`lig] **n.** 同事
8 responsibility [rɪ͵spɑnsə`bɪlətɪ] **n.** 責任

文法重點解析

解析重點 **1**

competitive

「competitive」這個字的意思有很多，都和「競爭」有關。例如你可以用它來表示「有競爭力的」，也可以用來表示「喜歡競爭的」、或「充滿競爭的」。在這封信中，它是用來表示「充滿競爭的」，也就是說在業務界競爭很激烈，要出頭並不容易。再來看看這個字的其他用法：

▶ She's very competitive. She doesn't back down from a challenge.
她很喜歡競爭，遇到挑戰絕不退縮。

▶ Their prices are quite competitive.
他們的價格很有競爭力（即很便宜）。

解析重點 **2**

lie before sb.

「lie before sb.」這個片語的意思直翻就是「躺在某人面前」。各種「責任」有可能躺在你面前嗎？責任又不是人，怎麼會「躺」在你面前？原來，信中此處是用這個片語來表示「這個人的面前有重重的責任」的意思，畢竟若我們把責任想像成人、把未來想像成一條道路，那麼要往前進的話，很難不被路上「躺著」的東西絆倒，不是嗎？再來看幾個例子：

▶ Many dangers lie before the team of explorers.
在這些探險家前面有著重重的危險。

▶ Countless challenges lie before us.
我們的面前有著重重的挑戰。

抄來抄去都抄這些！
補充例句

Unit
1

Unit
2

Unit
3

Unit
4

Unit
5

Unit
6

Unit
7

以下還有一些「恭賀升遷」常用的例句供參考，也可以活用在你的英文e-mail中喔！別忘了，時間、人名等等的地方要換成符合自己狀況的單字或句子。

❶ Congratulations on your promotion!
恭喜你升職！

❷ You definitely deserve this.
這真的是你應得的。

❸ I wish you every success in your new position.
我祝福你在新的崗位上一切順利成功。

❹ Please accept my warmest congratulations.
請接受我最熱烈的祝賀。

❺ I was extremely pleased to hear that you got promoted.
非常開心聽說你升職了。

❻ It's great to hear that you finally got what you deserved.
很開心聽說你終於得到應得的提拔了。

297

7-3 恭賀獲獎

From terry@mail.com
To martin@mail.com
Subject Congratulations on Winning the Award

Dear Martin,

I <u>can't be happier to</u> learn that you've won the annual [1] Outstanding [2] Employee Award [3], and I believe no one could have been more <u>deserving of</u> this title than you. Your hardworking attitude [4] combined [5] with your sincere [6] and friendly personality [7] made you highly esteemed [8] by all, including me.

I wish you continued success and a dynamic [9] future.

Affectionately [10],
Terry

打開光碟，複製貼上，
不用一分鐘，抄完一封信！

★套色的部分為關鍵單字 在右頁可以看到解釋喔！
★劃底線的部分都有相關的文法補充 請翻到下一頁就可以看到囉！

中文翻譯

Unit 1

Unit 2

Unit 3

Unit 4

Unit 5

Unit 6

Unit 7

親愛的馬丁：

得知您贏得年度傑出員工獎，我實在開心得不得了，我相信沒有人比你更值得這個獎。您努力工作的態度加上誠懇又友善的個性，使得您受到大家的高度肯定，包括我也一樣。

祝福您一切持續順利，未來生氣蓬勃。

誠摯地，
泰瑞

抄來抄去都抄這些！關鍵單字　　　　⊗□⊖

① annual [`ænjʊəl] **adj.** 年度的
② outstanding [`aʊt`stændɪŋ] **adj.** 傑出的
③ award [ə`wɔrd] **n.** 獎項
④ attitude [`ætətjud] **n.** 態度
⑤ combine [kəm`baɪn] **v.** 綜合，結合
⑥ sincere [sɪn`sɪr] **adj.** 誠摯的
⑦ personality [ˌpɝsn`ælətɪ] **n.** 個性，人格
⑧ esteem [ɪs`tim] **v.** 尊重，尊敬
⑨ dynamic [daɪ`næmɪk] **adj.**
　 有活力的，有生氣的
⑩ affectionately [ə`fɛkʃənɪtlɪ] **adv.** 親暱地

文法重點解析

解析重點 **1**
can't be happier to

這裡用了否定的「can't」，表示「不能更開心了」的意思。既然「不能更開心了」，那就是「開心到頂點、極致」，也就是「超級開心、開心得不得了」的意思啦！所以可別因為出現了否定的can't，就以為這是表示「不開心」的意思了。後面加了to，就表示「（做某事）非常開心」的意思。

解析重點 **2**
deserving of

deserving of是表達「值得（某事）」、「應得（某事）」的意思。deserve這個字很好用，不但可以拿來表達值得「好事」，也可以拿來表達值得「壞事」。就像我們中文也會說某人遇到壞事是「他應得的、他活該」不是嗎？來看幾個deserve的使用例：

▶ You're far too kind. I don't deserve such praise.
您太客氣了，我不值得這樣的稱讚。

▶ He got slapped by his girlfriend. I'd say he deserved it.
他被女朋友呼了一巴掌，我看這是他應得的。

抄來抄去都抄這些！
補充例句

Unit 1
Unit 2
Unit 3
Unit 4
Unit 5
Unit 6
Unit 7

以下還有一些「恭賀獲獎」常用的例句供參考，也可以活用在你的英文e-mail中喔！別忘了，時間、人名等等的地方要換成符合自己狀況的單字或句子。

❶ Congrats to the winner!
恭喜贏家！

❷ Congratulations on winning the big prize!
恭喜你得到了大獎！

❸ I'm excited to hear that you've been awarded the scholarship.
聽說你拿到了獎學金，我真是太興奮了。

❹ May I have some of your luck?
可以給我一點你的好運嗎？

❺ You totally deserve this award.
這個獎完全是你應得的。

❻ I've always thought that this award belongs to you and no one else.
我一直都覺得這個獎應該屬於你，不屬於任何其他人。

⊗ ⊡ ⊖

From don@mail.com
To catharine@mail.com
Subject **Congratulations on your Wedding!**

Dear Catharine,
I am thrilled [1] and delighted [2] to receive the invitation to your wedding. My wife joins me in expressing [3] our sincere congratulations and sends our best wishes. We will, of course, <u>be present</u> [4] at your wedding!

Have you decided on where your honeymoon will be yet? If not, we might have a few suggestions—my wife and I have <u>done quite a bit of research</u> [5] before we decided on our destination [6]!

Affectionately,
Don

打開光碟,複製貼上,
不用一分鐘,抄完一封信!

★套色的部分為關鍵單字 在右頁可以看到解釋喔!
★劃底線的部分都有相關的文法補充 請翻到下一頁就可以看到囉!

中文翻譯

親愛的凱薩琳：

得到您婚禮的邀請，我既興奮又開心。我太太與我一同表達我們誠摯的恭賀，也送上最美好的祝福。我們當然會去參加您的婚禮囉！

您已經決定蜜月要去哪裡了嗎？如果還沒，我們可以提供一些建議。我跟我太太在決定蜜月地點的時候可是好好研究了一番呢！

誠摯地，
堂恩

Unit 1
Unit 2
Unit 3
Unit 4
Unit 5
Unit 6
Unit 7

抄來抄去都抄這些！關鍵單字 ⊗ ▢ ⊖

❶ thrilled [θrɪld] adj. 興奮的
❷ delighted [dɪ`laɪtɪd] adj. 開心的
❸ express [ɪk`sprɛs] v. 表達
❹ present [`prɛznt] adj. 出席的，在場的
❺ research [rɪ`sɝtʃ] n. 研究，調查
❻ destination [ˌdɛstə`neʃən] n. 目的地

文法重點解析

解析重點1

be present at

大家可能知道，present當名詞的時候是「禮物」的意思，或也可以表達「現在」。而在片語be present at中，present是形容詞，意思則變成了「出席的、在場的」，也就是説，這封信中用了這個片語，即是表示「您的婚禮我們一定出席、一定到場」的意思。再來看幾個例子：

▶ There are only two adults present.
現場只有兩個成人。

▶ Several worried parents are present at the meeting.
許多憂慮的父母都出席會議。

解析重點2

do research

do research即「做研究」的意思，可是指的不完全是「做實驗」的那種研究喔！research比較偏向蒐集資料、或由已經有的數據中整理歸納出結論的那種「研究」。如果要説研究某個特定的主題，可以説「do research on（主題）」，看看以下例子：

▶ Let's do some research on customer preferences.
我們來研究一下消費者的偏好吧。

▶ My friend is doing research on ways to fight cancer.
我朋友在研究對付癌症的方式。

抄來抄去都抄這些！
補充例句

Unit 1
Unit 2
Unit 3
Unit 4
Unit 5
Unit 6
Unit 7

以下還有一些「恭賀新婚」常用的例句供參考，也可以活用在你的英文e-mail中喔！別忘了，時間、人名等等的地方要換成符合自己狀況的單字或句子。

❶ Congratulations on finally tying the knot!
　　恭喜你們終於要結婚了！

❷ You two are meant for each other.
　　你們真是天生一對。

❸ Please accept my congratulations on your marriage!
　　請接受我對你們婚姻最衷心的祝福！

❹ I wish you a happy life together.
　　祝你們一起度過快樂的生活。

❺ I am looking forward to attending your wedding in May.
　　期盼參加你們五月的婚禮。

❻ I've always thought you're perfect for each other.
　　我一直覺得你們非常適合對方。

⊗ ▣ ⊖

From steven@mail.com
To wilson@mail.com
Subject Congratulations on your Admission to University

Dear Wilson,

I was extremely ¹ happy when I learned that you have been admitted ² to Yale and I am writing to send my sincerest congratulations. I know that you have wanted this for many years and you've worked very hard towards your goal. I'm sure that you will do very well in your dream university ³!

I'll feel a bit lonely ⁴ after you're gone to your new school, but let's keep in touch, shall we?

Affectionately,
Steven

打開光碟，複製貼上，
不用一分鐘，抄完一封信！

★套色的部分為關鍵單字 在右頁可以看到解釋喔！
★劃底線的部分都有相關的文法補充 請翻到下一頁就可以看到囉！

中文翻譯

親愛的威爾森：

聽說你被耶魯大學錄取的消息，我非常高興，特別寫信向你致以我衷心的祝賀。我知道這是你多年來一直想要的事，而且你一直很努力朝著目標前進。相信你在你的夢想大學將會一切順利。

你去了新學校後，我會有點寂寞，但我們保持聯絡吧，好嗎？

誠摯地，
史蒂芬

Unit
1

Unit
2

Unit
3

Unit
4

Unit
5

Unit
6

Unit
7

抄來抄去都抄這些！關鍵單字　　　⊗ ☐ ⊖

❶ extremely [ɪk`strimlɪ] **adv.** 非常地

❷ admit [əd`mɪt] **v.** 承認

❸ university [ˌjunə`vɝsətɪ] **n.** 大學

❹ lonely [`lonlɪ] **adj.** 寂寞的

文法重點解析

解析重點 **1**

work towards

「work towards sth.」這個片語表達的是「朝著
（某個目標）努力」的意思，後面常搭配goal、
target之類的單字。來看幾個例子：

▶ You'll do well as long as you set a realistic goal
and work towards it.
只要你訂下一個實在的目標，朝著它努力，就
會一切順利的。

▶ We're working towards providing you all a
better work environment.
我們在努力要提供你們一個更好的工作環境。

解析重點 **2**

lonely

lonely雖然後面有個-ly，看起來像是副詞，但其實
它是形容詞，是用來修飾名詞的喔！和lonely長得
很像、也很容易搞混的一個形容詞是alone，兩者
的不同在於，lonely指的是「寂寞的」，alone則
是「單獨的，一個人的」。不能代換使用喔！畢
竟一個人的時候不見得會覺得寂寞，而就算不是
一個人也有可能會覺得寂寞。來看幾個例子：

▶ I felt so lonely when studying abroad.
我在國外唸書的時候感覺很寂寞。

▶ He prefers to be alone instead of being with a
lot of people.
他喜歡自己一個人，而不是跟很多人在一起。

抄來抄去都抄這些！
補充例句

Unit
1

Unit
2

Unit
3

Unit
4

Unit
5

Unit
6

Unit
7

以下還有一些「恭賀金榜題名」常用的例句供參考，也可以活用在你的英文e-mail中喔！別忘了，時間、人名等等的地方要換成符合自己狀況的單字或句子。

❶ Congratulations on your admission to your dream school!

恭喜你考上你夢想的學校！

❷ I just heard that you were accepted to your dream university.

我剛聽說你被你夢想中的大學錄取了。

❸ I'm sure that you will do just fine there.

我相信你在那裡會一切順利的。

❹ I'm sure you'll be an outstanding student there.

相信你在那裡會是個很傑出的學生。

❺ I'm so proud of you.

我很以你為傲。

❻ It's great to learn that your hard work has paid off.

很開心知道你的努力有了回報。

⊗▣⊖

From jenny@mail.com
To lisa@mail.com
Subject **Congratulations on Moving!**

Dear Lisa,

It's great that you finally have your own place after house-hunting for so long. It looks amazing [1] from the pictures! I especially adore [2] your bedroom with a nice view. I've always wanted a bedroom like that, but too bad mine faces a brick wall and my boyfriend's doesn't even have a window!

To celebrate [3] this occasion [4], I have bought a set of silverware [5] for you to use in your new shiny kitchen. Hope you like it! Best wishes to you and your family.

Affectionately,
Jenny

 打開光碟，複製貼上，
不用一分鐘，抄完一封信！

★套色的部分為關鍵單字 在右頁可以看到解釋喔！
★劃底線的部分都有相關的文法補充 請翻到下一頁就可以看到囉！

中文翻譯

親愛的麗莎：

在妳找房子找了這麼久之後終於有了自己的家，真是太棒了。從照片看起來真是超棒的！我尤其喜歡妳的臥室，景很不錯。我一直都想要這樣的臥室，可惜我的臥室窗戶面對一堵磚牆，而我男朋友的臥室連窗戶都沒有呢。

為了慶祝這件事，我買了一組銀製餐具讓妳在妳閃亮亮的新廚房裡使用。希望妳會喜歡！祝福妳與妳的家人。

誠摯地，
珍妮

Unit 1
Unit 2
Unit 3
Unit 4
Unit 5
Unit 6
Unit 7

抄來抄去都抄這些！關鍵單字　　　　⊗ ▢ ━

❶ amazing [ə`mezɪŋ] **adj.** 極好的，驚人的

❷ adore [ə`dor] **v.** 喜愛

❸ celebrate [`sɛlə͵bret] **v.** 慶祝

❹ occasion [ə`keʒən] **n.** 場合，活動

❺ silverware [`sɪlvɚ͵wɛr] **n.** 銀餐具

文法重點解析

house-hunting

「hunt」一般是「打獵」的意思，而我們在找房子的時候，不是也有點像打獵一樣，要仔細篩選適合的目標然後在被別人搶走之前把它弄到手嗎？因此找房子就可以稱為house-hunting了。除此之外，你也可以說apartment-hunting（找套房）、recruit-hunting（找新人）、job-hunting（找工作）等。如果你想要找一件好看的洋裝，也可以說I'm hunting for a new dress.（我在找一件新洋裝。）

shiny

shiny表示「閃亮的」的意思，很容易和長得很像的另一個形容詞「shining」搞混。兩者之間有什麼差別呢？原來，shining一般用來描述「自己會發光」的東西，例如太陽、燈等等；而像是錢幣、擦得發亮的鞋子等等都不是自己會發光的，而是會「反光」的東西，這些則可以用shiny來描述。這封信中，收信人家裡的廚房當然不是自己會發光的，而是反射了光線而看起來亮晶晶，因此選用shiny而不是shining來描述。

抄來抄去都抄這些！
補充例句

以下還有一些「恭賀喬遷」常用的例句供參考，也可以活用在你的英文e-mail中喔！別忘了，時間、人名等等的地方要換成符合自己狀況的單字或句子。

Unit
1

Unit
2

Unit
3

Unit
4

Unit
5

Unit
6

Unit
7

❶ Thank you for letting me know that you've moved.

謝謝你讓我知道你搬家了。

❷ Congratulations on finding your dream home!

恭喜你找到了你夢想中的家！

❸ I'd love to visit you someday.

我很想哪天去拜訪你。

❹ Here's a vase of flowers for your new house.

這是給妳新家裝飾用的一盆花。

❺ Your new house looks pretty great!

你的新家看起來好棒啊！

❻ I'm excited to hear that you've bought a house.

聽說你買了一棟房子，我很興奮。

313

7-7 恭賀新店開張

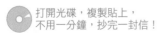

From edmund@mail.com
To marco@mail.com
Subject Congratulations on Opening a New Store!

Dear Marco,

I'm glad to hear that you've set up your own restaurant business, which has been in fact doing quite well. I've already read several good reviews [1] about your restaurant by some pretty well-known bloggers [2]! I bet customers [3] will be <u>pouring in</u> <u>in no time</u>.

I do hope your company enjoys a smooth [4] development [5] and wish you a flourishing [6] business!

Yours Faithfully,
Edmund

打開光碟，複製貼上，
不用一分鐘，抄完一封信！

★套色的部分為關鍵單字 在右頁可以看到解釋喔！
★劃底線的部分都有相關的文法補充 請翻到下一頁就可以看到囉！

中文翻譯

親愛的馬可：

很開心聽說您建立了自己的餐飲公司，目前也一切順利。我已經讀了幾篇部落客寫的評論，都給予您的餐廳正面評價。我看顧客肯定不久後就都會蜂擁而至了吧！

衷心希望您的公司發展順利，也祝福您生意興隆！

誠摯地，
愛德蒙

Unit 1

Unit 2

Unit 3

Unit 4

Unit 5

Unit 6

Unit 7

抄來抄去都抄這些！關鍵單字　　⊗□⊖

❶ review [rɪ`vju] n. 評論

❷ blogger [`blɔɡɚ] n. 部落客

❸ customer [`kʌstəmɚ] n. 顧客

❹ smooth [smuð] adj. 順利的，順暢的

❺ development [dɪ`vɛləpmənt] n. 發展

❻ flourish [`flɝɪʃ] v. 蓬勃發展

文法重點解析

pour in

片語「pour in」字面上的意思是「倒進」,像把水倒進杯子裡就可以說是「pour the water into the cup」。而大家可以想像,有很多水要「倒進」某個地方,這個狀況和很多人要「擠進」某個地方不是很像嗎?所以如果要表達有很多人潮著一個地方「蜂擁而入」,也可以用pour in來表達。就像我們中文也會把人譬喻成水,說「湧入」、「人潮」不是嗎?

解析重點 2

in no time

in no time直翻就是「在沒有時間之間」。這是什麼意思?其實就是「很快地」、「一眨眼之間」!來看幾個例子:

▶ The room filled up with students in no time.
眨眼之間房間裡就充滿了學生。

▶ Don't worry; I'll be back in no time.
不用擔心,我沒多久就會回來了。

抄來抄去都抄這些！
補充例句

Unit
1

Unit
2

Unit
3

Unit
4

Unit
5

Unit
6

Unit
7

以下還有一些「恭賀新店開張」常用的例
句供參考，也可以活用在你的英文e-mail中
喔！別忘了，時間、人名等等的地方要換成
符合自己狀況的單字或句子。

❶ I wish you success in your business!
祝福你生意興隆！

❷ May business prosper for you!
希望你生意興隆！

❸ I'm glad to hear that you've opened a
boutique.
很開心聽到你開了一家精品店。

❹ I'll definitely drop by your store.
我一定會去拜訪你的店的。

❺ You'll make an excellent store manager.
你肯定會是個很好的店面主管。

❻ I promise to visit your new store soon.
我保證不久後一定會去拜訪你的新店。

❼ Give your old friend (me) a discount, won't you?
給你的老朋友（也就是我）打個折吧，好不好？

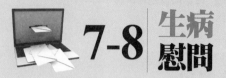
⊗◻⊖

From john@mail.com
To jackson@mail.com
Subject Get Well Soon!

Dear Jackson,

I'm sorry to hear that you had had to undergo [1] an operation [2] on your leg. I hope that <u>by the time</u> this E-mail reaches you, you're already feeling <u>a great deal</u> better. I'm sure that it won't be long before you're entirely [3] and completely [4] yourself again.

Everyone here at the office misses you and wishes you a speedy [5] recovery [6].

Yours Faithfully,
John

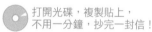

打開光碟，複製貼上，
不用一分鐘，抄完一封信！

★套色的部分為關鍵單字 在右頁可以看到解釋喔！
★劃底線的部分都有相關的文法補充 請翻到下一頁就可以看到囉！

中文翻譯

親愛的傑克森，

很遺憾聽說您得動腿部手術。我希望到您收到這封電子郵件的時候，您已經感覺好多了。相信不久後您就會完全復原了。

辦公室的大家都很想您，希望您能盡快康復。

誠摯地，
約翰

Unit 1
Unit 2
Unit 3
Unit 4
Unit 5
Unit 6
Unit 7

抄來抄去都抄這些！關鍵單字   ✕ ☐ ━

❶ undergo [ˌʌndɚˋgo] **v.** 經歷，忍受
❷ operation [ˌɑpəˋreʃən] **n.** 手術
❸ entirely [ɪnˋtaɪrlɪ] **adv.** 完全地
❹ completely [kəmˋplitlɪ] **adv.** 完全地
❺ speedy [ˋspidɪ] **adj.** 快速的
❻ recovery [rɪˋkʌvərɪ] **n.** 復原

文法重點解析

解析重點1
by the time

「by the time」這個片語的意思是「到……的時候」，用在這封信中此處即是表示「到了你收到這封信的時候」。我們再看幾個例子：

▶ By the time you arrive, everyone will already be asleep.

等你到達的時候，大家都要睡著了。

▶ By the time he got home, his whole family had already gone out.

等他到家的時候，他全家人都已經出門了。

解析重點2
a great deal

片語「a great deal」指的即是「很多」的意思，例如在這封信中就是指「感覺好很多」的意思。再看幾個例子：

▶ He always makes a great deal of noise in the morning.

他每天早上總是發出很多聲音。

▶ He made a great deal of money last year.

他去年賺了很多錢。

抄來抄去都抄這些！
補充例句

Unit
1

Unit
2

Unit
3

Unit
4

Unit
5

Unit
6

Unit
7

以下還有一些「生病慰問」常用的例句供參
考，也可以活用在你的英文e-mail中喔！別
忘了，時間、人名等等的地方要換成符合自
己狀況的單字或句子。

❶ I'm sorry to hear that you're ill.
聽到你生病了，我很遺憾。

❷ I hope you get well soon.
希望你盡快好起來。

❸ I'll be praying for your swift recovery.
我會祈禱你盡快康復。

❹ I'm sure you'll be up and about in no time.
你一定可以很快復原的。

❺ Everyone misses you and hope you'll be
back soon.
大家都很想你，希望你能趕快回來。

❻ Please have a good rest.
請好好休息。

❼ Do take care of yourself and your own health.
請好好照顧自己與自己的健康。

⊗ ▢ ⊖

From simon@mail.com
To dan@mail.com
Subject Sorry to Hear about your Accident

Dear Dan,

I'm sorry to hear that you were in a car accident [1] yesterday. How are you feeling now? I wish I could visit you, but apparently [2] only family members are allowed in right now. I promise I'll swing by with some fruit and games later when the nurses give me the okay.

I wish you a quick recovery [3]! I can't wait till you get better and we can spend the rest of our summer vacation hanging out at the swimming pool.

Yours Faithfully [4],
Simon

打開光碟，複製貼上，
不用一分鐘，抄完一封信！

★套色的部分為關鍵單字 在右頁可以看到解釋喔！
★劃底線的部分都有相關的文法補充 請翻到下一頁就可以看到囉！

中文翻譯

親愛的丹尼：

很遺憾聽説你昨天出了車禍。你現在感覺如何？我真希望可以去拜訪你，但看來目前只有家人可以進去。我保證等護士説可以以後，我會帶一些水果和遊戲去找你。

早日康復喔！我等不及你趕快恢復了，我們可以一起在游泳池閒晃度過暑假剩下的時間。

誠摯地，
賽門

Unit 1
Unit 2
Unit 3
Unit 4
Unit 5
Unit 6
Unit 7

抄來抄去都抄這些！關鍵單字   ⊗ ◻ ⊜

❶ accident [`æksədənt] **n.** 意外

❷ apparently [ə`pærəntlɪ] **adv.** 明顯地，顯然

❸ recovery [rɪ`kʌvərɪ] **n.** 復原，康復

❹ faithfully [`feθfəlɪ] **adv.** 忠誠地

文法重點解析

解析重點1
swing by

「swing by」這個片語的意思是「經過（某處）並短暫地進去」，是個比較口語的用法，用在這封信中此處即是表示「順便經過你的病房，進去探望一下你」的意思。我們再看幾個例子：

► You're welcome to swing by my place.
歡迎你來我家拜訪一下。

► We swung by the supermarket to pick up some beer. 我們順便進去超市買一些啤酒。

解析重點2
give sb. the okay

片語「give 某人 the okay」直翻就是「給某人一個OK」，也就是「同意某人（做某事）」的意思啦！例如在這封信中就是指「護士一旦同意我進去看你，我就會帶著水果跟遊戲進去了」的意思。再看幾個例子：

► We're waiting for him to give us the okay before surprising her with the birthday cake.
我們在等他給我們OK的信號，然後才能拿生日蛋糕進去給她驚喜。

► I can't sign this unless my boss gives me the okay.
如果我老闆不同意我簽，我就不能簽。

抄來抄去都抄這些！
補充例句

Unit
1

Unit
2

Unit
3

Unit
4

Unit
5

Unit
6

Unit
7

以下還有一些「遭逢意外慰問」常用的例句供參考，也可以活用在你的英文e-mail中喔！別忘了，時間、人名等等的地方要換成符合自己狀況的單字或句子。

❶ I'm sorry to hear that you were hit by a car.
很遺憾聽説你被車撞了。

❷ I hope you'll be up and walking in no time.
希望你不久後就可以起來到處走動了。

❸ I was so relieved to hear that your injury isn't serious.
聽到你傷得不重，我真是鬆了一口氣。

❹ If you get bored in the hospital, just tell me and I'll visit you.
你如果在醫院很無聊，跟我説，我會去拜訪你。

❺ I can smuggle some videogames into your hospital room if you like.
如果你想要，我可以偷渡一些電動到你的病房裡。

❻ Please take care of yourself.
請好好照顧自己。

⊗◎●

From colin@mail.com
To will@mail.com
Subject Sorry to Hear about the Earthquake

Dear Will,

I'm dreadfully [1] sorry to hear that your house was destroyed [2] in the earthquake [3] last week.

I understand that this must be a difficult time for you and you might not have a lot of time for E-mails, but I just want to write and let you know that we're all here for you, and please feel free to ask if you need any help. If there's anything you and your family need, just let us know and we'll do our best to provide you what we can. It's what friends are for, right?

Yours Faithfully,
Colin

打開光碟,複製貼上,
不用一分鐘,抄完一封信!

★套色的部分為關鍵單字 在右頁可以看到解釋喔!
★劃底線的部分都有相關的文法補充 請翻到下一頁就可以看到囉!

Unit 1
Unit 2
Unit 3
Unit 4
Unit 5
Unit 6
Unit 7

中文翻譯

親愛的威爾，
聽說你的家在上禮拜的地震中毀了，我非常遺憾。

我明白這段時間對你而言肯定很難熬，也知道你可能沒什麼時間寫電子郵件，但我還是想寫信告訴你，我們都在這裡陪著你，如果需要幫忙的話也可以儘管找我們。如果你或你的家人需要什麼東西，儘管讓我們知道，我們會盡我們所能提供你們幫助。這是朋友該做的嘛，不是嗎？

誠摯地，
科林

抄來抄去都抄這些！關鍵單字　⊗ ▢ ⊖

❶ dreadfully [`drɛdfəlɪ] **adv.** 非常地，糟糕地
❷ destroy [dɪ`strɔɪ] **v.** 毀滅，毀掉
❸ earthquake [`ɝθˌkwek] **n.** 地震

文法重點解析

解析重點 1

be here for sb.

「be here for sb.」這個片語的意思是「在這裡陪著（某人）」，通常用於有人遇到了慘事需要安慰的時候，是個非常好用的片語。用在這封信中即是表示「我知道你可能忙得沒空理我們，但如果你需要，我們一直都在」的意思。此外也可以說成「be there for sb.」我們再看幾個例子：

▶ If anything happens, I'll be there for you.
　　無論發生什麼事，我都會陪著你。

▶ Don't be scared; we're here for you.
　　不用怕，我們都在這裡陪著你呢。

解析重點 2

feel free to

片語「feel free to」直翻就是「覺得可以自由地（做某事）」，其實也就是「不用顧忌，盡量（做某事）」的意思啦！例如在這封信中就是指「有需要儘管找我，不用顧忌」。再看幾個例子：

▶ Feel free to give me a call if you need help.
　　需要幫忙的話儘管打給我。

▶ Please feel free to send me all your questions.
　　請儘管把你的疑問都告知我。

抄來抄去都抄這些！
補充例句

Unit 1

Unit 2

Unit 3

Unit 4

Unit 5

Unit 6

Unit 7

以下還有一些「遭逢天災事故慰問」常用的例句供參考，也可以活用在你的英文e-mail中喔！別忘了，時間、人名等等的地方要換成符合自己狀況的單字或句子。

❶ I'm shocked to hear what happened.
聽到發生了什麼事，我真的很震撼。

❷ I will do all I can to help you rebuild your home.
我會盡全力幫助你重建家園。

❸ If you need anything, just ask.
如果你需要什麼，盡管找我吧。

❹ I'm really sorry to hear about the fire.
聽說火災的事我很遺憾。

❺ Please remember that we'll always be by your side.
請記得，我們會一直在你身旁。

❻ No matter what happens, you'll still have us.
無論發生什麼事，你還有我們啊。

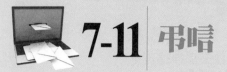

⊗▢⊖

From topher@mail.com
To randy@mail.com
Subject Offering my Full Sympathy

Dear Randy,

The news of your brother's death [1] shocked [2] me. Please accept my deepest sympathies [3]. I've known him for many years, and I must say that he was an intelligent [4], kind-hearted [5] and just [6] man. I'm sure everyone will miss him a great deal.

Please convey [7] my deepest sympathy to your family.

Yours Faithfully,
Topher

 打開光碟，複製貼上，
不用一分鐘，抄完一封信！

★套色的部分為關鍵單字 在右頁可以看到解釋喔！
★劃底線的部分都有相關的文法補充 請翻到下一頁就可以看到囉！

中文翻譯

親愛的蘭迪：

你哥哥的死讓我非常震撼。請接受我最深的同情。我已經認識他許多年了，我必須說，他是個聰明、善良又正直的人。相信每個人都會非常想念他的。

請代我向你的家人傳達我最深切的慰問。

誠摯地，
托佛

Unit 1
Unit 2
Unit 3
Unit 4
Unit 5
Unit 6
Unit 7

抄來抄去都抄這些！關鍵單字 ⊗ ◻ ⊖

❶ death [dɛθ] **n.** 死亡
❷ shock [ʃɑk] **v.** 使驚嚇，使震撼
❸ sympathy [`sɪmpəθɪ] **n.** 同情
❹ intelligent [ɪn`tɛlədʒənt] **adj.** 聰明的，機智的
❺ kind-hearted [kaɪnd-`hɑrtɪd] **adj.** 善良的
❻ just [dʒʌst] **adj.** 正義的
❼ convey [kən`ve] **v.** 傳達

文法重點解析

解析重點 1

shocked

「shock」是一個用途很多的單字，不但可以表示「觸電」，還可以拿來表達「驚訝」、「驚嚇」的意思。不過要注意的是，shock可不是指一般程度的驚訝而已，而是非常嚴重、震撼的驚訝。例如若只是走在路上有貓跑出來被嚇了一跳，那就不能説「shocked」，而如果你一直以為你的朋友是男的，但她其實是女的，這可就是非常驚訝的事，可以用「shocked」來形容。來看幾個例子：

▶ I was shocked to learn that he was actually forty instead of twenty. 我發現他不是二十歲而是四十歲，真是超驚訝的。

▶ He got shocked when plugging his computer in. 他在幫電腦插電的時候觸電了。

解析重點 2

I must say that...

「I must say that...」是一個很好用的句型，帶有「我不得不説……」的含意。像是在這封信中，就是用來表示「你的哥哥實在太聰明、太善良、太正直，所以我不得不稱讚他」的意思。再看幾個例子：

▶ I must say that I'm very impressed with your work. 我不得不説，你的作品讓我印象非常深刻。

▶ I must say that you're one of the best artists I've ever met. 我不得不説，你是我遇過最好的一個藝術家。

抄來抄去都抄這些！
補充例句

Unit
1

Unit
2

Unit
3

Unit
4

Unit
5

Unit
6

Unit
7

以下還有一些「弔唁」常用的例句供參考，也可以活用在你的英文e-mail中喔！別忘了，時間、人名等等的地方要換成符合自己狀況的單字或句子。

❶ The news of his death was a terrible shock to us.
他過世的噩耗讓我們非常震驚。

❷ I am sorry to hear that he has passed away.
聽到他過世，我非常遺憾。

❸ I am deeply grieved to hear about this news.
聽到這個消息，我非常遺憾。

❹ I am so sorry about your loss.
對於失去這麼好的人，我非常遺憾。

❺ I will really miss him very much.
我會非常想念他的。

❻ Everyone who has known him must have felt a great loss.
他的過世對所有認識他的人來說都是個很大的損失。

原來如此 系列 E141

抄來抄去都抄這些！
生活必用英文E-mail—30秒抄完一封信

30秒抄完一封英文E-mail，就是有這麼簡單！

作　　者	李宇凡	
顧　　問	曾文旭	
總 編 輯	王毓芳	
編輯統籌	耿文國、黃璽宇	
主　　編	吳靜宜、張辰安	
美術編輯	王桂芳、王文璇	
行銷企劃	許之芸	
法律顧問	北辰著作權事務所　蕭雄淋律師、嚴裕欽律師	

印　　製	世和印製企業有限公司
初　　版	2016年05月
出　　版	捷徑文化出版事業有限公司
電　　話	（02）6636-8398
傳　　真	（02）6636-8397
地　　址	106 台北市大安區忠孝東路四段218-7號7樓

定　　價	新台幣360元／港幣120元
產品內容	1書+1光碟

總 經 銷	采舍國際有限公司
地　　址	235 新北市中和區中山路二段366巷10號3樓
電　　話	（02）8245-8786
傳　　真	（02）8245-8718

港澳地區總經銷	和平圖書有限公司
地　　址	香港柴灣嘉業街12號百樂門大廈17樓
電　　話	（852）2804-6687
傳　　真	（852）2804-6409

捷徑 Book站

現在就上臉書（FACEBOOK）「捷徑BOOK站」並按讚加入粉絲團，
就可享每月不定期新書資訊和粉絲專享小禮物喔！
http://www.facebook.com/royalroadbooks
讀者來函：royalroadbooks@gmail.com

國家圖書館出版品預行編目資料

抄來抄去都抄這些! 生活必用英文E-mail—
30秒抄完一封信 / 李宇凡著. -- 初版.
-- 臺北市 : 捷徑文化, 2016.05
面；　公分（原來如此：E141）

ISBN 978-986-5698-95-9(平裝)

1. 英語　2. 電子郵件　3. 應用文

805.179　　　　　　　　　　105004002